"This has got to stop," she stated at last

Sam eased the Bentley to a gentler pace before replying. "There are some things that cannot be stopped, Polly. The tides of the sea, the changing seasons...love. Have you ever been in love, Polly?"

"Once," she told him soberly—and didn't add, for all time, because she knew she would never love anyone quite as she loved him. When he was married to Deidre, Polly would make herself get over it. Without meaning to, she sighed out loud, "Oh, you must get married soon, Sam."

He laughed softly. "Oh, I intend to."

Sam pulled onto the side of the road and leaned over to kiss her, not mildly at all. Then he drove on at once, whistling under his breath, while Polly sat wordlessly beside him.

Books by Betty Neels

Polly

Betty Neels

Harlequin Books

TORONTO • NEW YORK • LONDON
AMSTERDAM • PARIS • SYDNEY • HAMBURG
STOCKHOLM • ATHENS • TOKYO • MILAN

Original hardcover edition published in 1984
by Mills & Boon Limited

ISBN 0-373-02656-0

Harlequin Romance first edition November 1984

CHAPTER ONE

THE girl at the table read her letter slowly, her neat brown head bowed over its single page, watched by everyone sitting with her. She came to the end and then started to read it over again, and the boy sitting beside her cried impatiently: 'Polly, what's it say? Do tell us, why . . .'

'Hush, Ben.' His mother, even more impatient than he was, spoke quietly. 'Polly will tell us when she's ready.' She added hopefully: 'Won't you, dear?'

The girl looked up and glanced round—they were all there, her mother, father, two very pretty sisters and the twelve-year-old Ben. 'I've got the job,' she said, and beamed at them all in turn as she handed the letter to her father. 'Nine to five except Saturdays and Sundays and fifty pounds a week.'

'Darling, that's marvellous!' exclaimed her mother, smiling at her youngest daughter—the plain one of the family and the one with the brains. Cora and Marian had no need of brains; they were so pretty that they would marry just as soon as they could decide which of their numerous boy-friends would make the best husband. Ben was still at school and clever too, but it was Polly, twenty years old, with a clutch of O-levels and A-levels and a natural bent for dead languages, who had inherited her learned schoolmaster father's clever head. And a good thing too, thought Mrs Talbot, for she had no looks to speak of—a slightly turned up nose, far too wide a mouth, even though it had soft curves, straight brown hair and a little too plump for her medium height. Her only good features were her eyes, large and brown, fringed by curling lashes which needed no mascara at all. They twinkled engagingly now. 'It's a lot of money,' she said happily, and indeed for the Talbot family it was for there wasn't a great deal to spare by the time Ben's school fees had been paid and the rambling Victorian villa they lived in, with its elderly plumbing and draughts, was always in need of some vital repair or other. True, Cora and Marian both had jobs, cycling to nearby Pulchester, one to work in the public library on three afternoons a week, the other to spend her mornings in one of the town's boutiques. She was paid a pittance, but she was allowed to buy her clothes there at a big discount and naturally enough all her money went on that, and since she and Cora were the same size and shape, she bought for her too, so that neither of them ever had a penny piece between them. But at least, as Mrs Talbot pointed out to her husband, they paid for their clothes and perhaps they would be able to find better jobs later on. Or marry, she added to herself hopefully.

'When do you start, dear?' asked Mrs Talbot.

'Next Monday.' Polly drew her straight brows together. 'I'll have to leave at half past eight, won't I? It's twenty minutes on the bike if I do go down Tansy Lane.'

'What will you wear?' asked Cora.

Polly pondered for a moment. 'A skirt and a blouse, I suppose, and a cardigan. It'll be a bit chilly in the morning . . .'

'Ne'er cast a clout till May be out,' quoted Ben.

Polly grinned at him. 'Silly—it's April for another two weeks. I must pop over to see the Vicar and borrow his Greek dictionary; Shylock had the last few pages of mine.'

And presently, closeted with that learned gentleman, she explained why she needed it. 'Sir Ronald Wise,' she explained, raising her quiet voice a few tones in order to counteract his deafness. 'He wanted someone to type his book—a very learned one comparing Ancient Greek and Latin as languages, you know. And of course it'll be quicker if he has someone who understands a bit about it. I saw his advert in *The Times* and applied, and I've got the job.'

The Reverend Mr Mortimer nodded his bald head. 'That is excellent news, my dear. Your father must be proud of you.'

He fetched the dictionary. 'I shall be dining with Sir Ronald next week, he will doubtless tell me how you are getting on.'

Polly left him presently, did a little shopping at the village stores for her mother and started for home. The house was a little way out of the village, halfway up a short steep hill, beside a lane which wound its way in a nonchalant fashion to the next village. She wandered up it, not hurrying, for the spring sunshine was warm and her basket heavy. She was almost home when a Range Rover came over the brow of the hill and stopped squarely in the middle of the lane, leaving her no room to pass, and its driver addressed her.

'Wells Court—Sir Ronald Wise's place?' He was polite, but he was also in a towering rage; that she could see easily enough. He was very good-looking too, in a dark, beaky-nosed fashion. Polly studied his face. Everyone knew everyone else in her part of the world; this man was a stranger.

Prepared to be friendly and in no hurry at all, she observed: 'Good morning. Are you lost? People will take the short cut from Pulchester, you know, it looks so easy on the map, but if you don't know your way around it's twice as long.'

His politeness was icy now. 'I should be obliged if you would spare me your observations on rural communications. I realise that living in these— er—rustic conditions, time is not of paramount importance to you, but it is to me. Wells Court, if you would be so good . . .'

Polly gave him a pitying look. Poor man, in a rage about nothing, and in such a hurry, too. 'You need a rest and a cup of coffee,' she said kindly. 'I daresay you've come a long way. Turn left at the bottom of this lane, cross the village square and into the lane beside the church. Wells Court is a mile along the road—you can't miss it.' She added a friendly goodbye.

His own goodbye held more than a hint of mockery, but she didn't see that.

She forgot all about him in the small bustle of preparation for the new job, and when Monday morning came she set out on her bike, very neat in her navy pleated skirt, one of Cora's blouses, a little too big but very suitable with its prim round collar and silky bow under her chin, and her own cardigan would do very nicely, as she wouldn't need to wear it in the house.

She parked the bike beside the imposing front door and rang the bell. She knew the man who opened it by sight, for he went to church and sat in the pew reserved for Wells Court, but if he recognised her, he gave no sign. His, 'Miss Talbot?

You are expected,' was uttered in a voice devoid of expression, although he frowned slightly at the sight of the bicycle. 'I will ask the gardener's boy to put your bicycle in the shed at the side, miss,' he told her austerely, and stood aside for her to go in.

She had been in the house on one or two occasions; when it had been opened to the general public in aid of some charity or other, but never further than the entrance hall and the big reception rooms on either side. Now she followed the man along a passage at the back of the hall and waited while he tapped on a door at the end of it.

Sir Ronald's rather fruity voice bade them enter and Polly did so, slipping neatly past her guide, who shut the door behind her, leaving her to cross a broad expanse of polished floor to the desk at the far end of the room where Sir Ronald was seated.

'Ah, good morning, young lady. What's your name? Talbot?'

'Yes, Sir Ronald. Polly Talbot.'

'Yes, yes, of course. I've met your father somewhere—clever chap.' He glanced up at her, standing composedly in front of the desk. 'Got a couple of pretty sisters, haven't you?' He chuckled. 'But you've got the brains, eh?'

She wondered if this was a compliment. She said calmly: 'It's just that I like Greek and Latin. Sir Ronald, I'm not clever at anything else.' She almost added: 'And not pretty either,' but decided against it.

'Well, there's plenty of work for you, Polly. I've finished the glossary and it needs careful checking as you go along.' He leaned back in his chair and rather belatedly invited her to sit down. 'Greek and Latin,' he told her with some smugness, 'a comparison, if I may so describe it—as far as I know, there's been precious little written about the subject since Beeton's Classical Dictionary, although my work is no dictionary.' He turned to nod over one shoulder. 'There's a desk and typewriter and all you may need through there. You can start as soon as you wish.'

Polly got to her feet. 'Is there a time limit?' she asked.

'What? The publishers want it as soon as possible. You had better let me know how you're getting on at the end of the week. Now . . .' He fussed with some papers on his desk, and she prudently went through the door he had indicated and shut it quietly behind her.

The room was small and little used, she judged, but there was a fair-sized desk in it with a comfortable chair, a typewriter and a stack of paper and carbons, and of course the manuscript. She sat down and began to read it slowly. The first chapter was written in English and merely detailed the contents of the book. Without looking further, she typed it out; it took her most of the day with a break for coffee and then lunch, which were brought to her there on a tray. A friendly maid led her through a door back into the hall and showed her a downstairs cloakroom, and she lingered a while, glad of a chance to move around a little. The house was very quiet as she strolled round the hall, wishing she dared to go outside for ten minutes; tomorrow she would ask . . .

She finished the chapter by four o'clock, and since there was still an hour to go, she began to study the second chapter. A very different kettle of fish, she was soon to discover. Sir Ronald had plunged deeply into his subject, and although she was confident that she could type it correctly she had very little idea of what he was getting at. A tray of tea was a welcome relief, and presently, her day's work done, she laid her work on the desk in the study, and went into the hall. Someone would have to be told she was leaving; she was wondering who when the maid came through the service door at the back.

'I'm going home now,' said Polly. 'My bike's been put in a shed . . . can I get it?'

'You wait there, miss, it'll be fetched for you.' The girl went away again and Polly sat down in one of the massive chairs ranged against the wall. A cold unlived-in house, she decided, looking around her, probably because Sir Ronald was a widower with grown-up children living away from him. It was nice to get out into the garden again, jump on her bike and cycle home through the quiet lane.

Going in through the kitchen door presently, she could smell hot buttered toast and the wood fire in the sitting room and gave a contented sigh. Never mind the shabby furniture and the threadbare carpet in the hall—this was home, warm and welcoming. She washed her hands at the kitchen sink and hurried to the sitting room where the family were gathered round the fire having tea.

Her mother looked up as she went in. 'Darling—just in time, how nice. Did you have a good day?'

Polly took a great bite of buttery toast. 'I think so. The first bit's easy; I just had time to look at the next chapter and that's going to be a bit tricky, but I like it.'

She answered a string of questions, helped clear

the tea things and offered to take Shylock for his walk. Cora and Marian were both going out that evening and Ben had a pile of homework, so, as so often happened, Polly took the dog out far more often than anyone else; her sisters went out a good deal in the evening and could never find the time. And Shylock was a large unwieldy dog who needed a good deal of exercise. The pair of them went off happily, walking briskly in the chill of the spring evening, Shylock's large woolly head full of the pleasure of rabbit hunting, Polly's happily occupied with the delights of having money to spend.

But before that she had to work for it, and work hard. She was not unfamiliar with the Greek and the Latin so that she was able to keep at a fair speed—all the same, it took her three days to type the second chapter. She laid it before Sir Ronald halfway through the morning and sighed with relief when he glanced through it with evident satisfaction.

'Very nice, very nice, Polly. I shall go through it carefully later today. You have started the next chapter?' Without waiting for her to reply he added: 'You have all you want, I hope? Your meals and so on?'

'Yes, thank you, Sir Ronald. Would you mind if I went into the garden for a few minutes during my lunch break?' She hesitated. 'It will take me longer to type the rest of the book, Sir Ronald; I have to study each page . . .'

He nodded. 'Of course. Just so long as it's well done. There's no time limit, Polly.' He added to contradict himself: 'As soon as possible, you understand?'

He waved a vague hand at her, and she went

back to her desk and spent an hour frowning over the next chapter.

Lunch was a welcome break; she ate it quickly and hurried into the garden, to sit on a sheltered seat and feel the midday warmth of the sun on her face, and presently went back to work. It dealt with Greek and Latin proper names with a long explanation of the vowel sounds; she was halfway through this when the door opened and the driver of the Range Rover walked in. He looked at her with surprise. 'Good God, the rustic chatterbox! I'm looking for Miss Talbot.'

'Me,' said Polly, her colour heightened and her voice tart. She was neither rustic nor a chatterbox; he was insufferably rude, whoever he was.

He crossed the little room and leaned against the desk, a large, very tall man. 'Well, well, as my nanny so often remarked, wonders will never cease. Are you the paragon who's typing Sir Ronald's manuscript?'

'I am not a paragon, nor am I a rustic chatterbox. I'm typing his work, yes. Why do you want to know?'

Polly poised her hands over the keys in the hope that he would take the hint and go away. A friend of Sir Ronald's, she supposed, indulging in idle curiosity. She thought it unlikely that he would answer her question, and she was right, he ignored it completely, just went on standing there looking at her. 'You don't mind if I get on?' she asked frostily. 'I daresay someone will find Sir Ronald if you want to see him . . .'

The gentleman in question came through the door as she spoke, already talking. 'There you are, Sam. Been having a look at the manuscript, have you? Polly's doing a good job of the typing. A clever girl, is Polly—it isn't everyone who can read both Latin and Greek and type them intelligently as well.' He beamed at her. 'And that reminds me that your wages are on my desk, collect them as you go, will you?'

He took the other man by the arm. 'There's a most interesting book I want you to look at,' he told him as they walked to the door. 'I found it in Pulchester of all places, in a poky secondhand shop . . .' His voice faded as he went through the door, followed by his companion. Neither of them took any notice of Polly. She hadn't expected them to do so.

It was at the end of the afternoon, her wages safely stowed in her pocket, wheeling her bicycle away from the house, that Polly encountered the man again. He came out of the shrubbery bordering the long drive just as she was about to pedal away.

'Going home?' he asked idly. 'You live in the village?'

'Yes,' she answered politely. 'Good evening.'

She rode off fast, anxious to get away from him. She wasn't likely to see him again; the Range Rover had been parked on the sweep before the house, ready for him to leave. She wondered who he was and where he lived and why he was so abrupt in his manner. 'Downright rude,' she said out loud, then forgot him in the pleasure of deciding what she would do with the money in her pocket. There was, she estimated, about six weeks' work ahead of her, perhaps two months. She could save it up, of course, and have an orgy of spending at the end—on the other hand, she needed some new clothes and she could buy Ben the football boots he wanted for his birthday, and give her mother some housekeeping money too. She had made up her mind to that by the time she reached home; she could save something each week, and perhaps visit Aunt Maggie's in Scotland when she had finished.

Over tea she put these plans forward. Her offer of the boots was received with enthusiasm by her brother, just as the housekeeping money was welcomed in a more restrained manner by her mother. Her sisters, considering these to be unimportant, embarked at once on a deep discussion as to the clothes she should buy. It was soon evident to Polly that if she took their advice she would be penniless in no time at all and the possessor of more clothes than she would ever wear. But she didn't say so; Cora and Marian were helping her in their own way. She murmured suitably each time they paused to look at her and finally, when they had run out of ideas, suggested that it might be a good idea if she saved a few weeks' wages before she went shopping. 'For I'll not have time to wear anything much until I've finished the job,' she pointed out reasonably, and was relieved when they reluctantly agreed.

The weekend, with its well tried routine, came and went. A long walk with Shylock, time spent helping Ben with his homework and pottering round the house doing small chores for her mother, a little gardening, a pleasant half hour with her father, discussing Greek mythology. Cora and Marian were out, but they mostly were on Saturdays, driving somewhere or other with whichever boy-friend was in favour. They were out again on Sunday too, but only after they had gone to church with the rest of the family. Mr Talbot, a mild man, was adamant about that. They walked through the quiet village and filled the family pew, exchanging nods and smiles with the familiar faces around them. Polly, her head round the other way while she listened to a friend's gossip offered in a decorous whisper, almost had her ribs caved in by her sisters each side of her. 'Polly, who's that marvellous man, just come in with Sir Ronald? Have you seen him? Is he staying with him? Where does he come from?'

'I don't know, and yes, I've seen him. I suppose he's staying at Wells Court. I don't know where he's from.'

Two pairs of eyes stared at her in astonishment. 'You mean to say,' hissed Cora, 'that you've actually spoken to him and you don't know anything about him?' She was prevented from saying more because old Mr Symes, the organist, had stopped his gentle meandering over the keys and had begun the opening hymn as Mr Mortimer and his choir came out of the vestry.

It was at the end of the service, as Sir Ronald and his guest passed the Talbot pew and the former exchanged civil greetings with their father, that Cora and Marian had a chance to get a look at his companion.

A look he returned with some interest, for they were really very pretty and worth more than a glance. The look he gave Polly was quite another thing; it made her feel like yesterday's left-over cold potatoes.

There was no sign of him when she arrived at Wells Court on Monday morning, and indeed, for the moment she had forgotten him; it was a lovely day and the quiet Gloucestershire countryside was green and alive with the familiar sounds she had grown up with; lambs and sheep, cows lowing over

the hedges, tractors going to and fro, the birds . . .
She parked her bike and rang the bell.

The third chapter was to do with Greek and
Roman chronology. Polly was typing, very
carefully, the data concerning the Greek calendar
when Sir Ronald walked in, and his guest with
him. Their good mornings were affable as they
stood behind her chair, looking over her shoulder
at what she had already done. 'Munychlon',
observed Sir Ronald, 'so much better sounding
than April, don't you think? You've been to
Munychia, of course, Sam?'

'Yes. Does Miss—er—Talbot take an interest in
such things, or is she merely a typist?'

Rude! thought Polly, and said with commendable restraint. 'The festival of Munychia was held
in the town of that name, in honour of the goddess
Diana.' She added kindly: 'I believe that quite
ordinary people read about such things, Mr—
er . . .'

Sir Ronald coughed. 'Professor, my dear.
Professor Gervis. He's famous in his field, you
know.'

She raised guileless brown eyes. 'Indeed? What
field?'

The professor let out a bellow of laughter. 'I
don't often make mistakes,' he observed coolly,
'but with you I certainly did.' He turned away,
suddenly bored. 'Would it be a good idea if we
phoned Rogers this morning—there's the question
of the right type setting . . .'

Polly was left sitting there; she should have been
feeling triumphant, but she felt rather silly. She
must have sounded like a little prig; no wonder
he'd laughed!

She was sitting in the sun during her lunch

break when he appeared suddenly and sat down beside her. He asked without preamble: 'Have you never been away from the village? Surely with your talents you could have got a place at a university or found a well paid job with a museum or some such thing?'

She turned to look at him. 'I expect I could, only I haven't wanted to. I like the country; there's a lot more to do than just typing Greek and Latin . . .'

'You're not interested in money? It buys pretty clothes and pays for hairdressers and all the other things girls want.' The faint mockery in his voice annoyed her.

'Of course I like pretty things—even we rustics dress up occasionally. I daresay if I'd been born and brought up in some big city, I'd feel differently about it.'

'Those were your sisters in church?' he wanted to know idly.

'Yes.'

'Very pretty girls, and dressed charmingly.'

'Yes,' she got up, 'but as you see they're, as you say, very pretty girls. It's time I was back working. Goodbye.'

He went with her most annoyingly into the house. As he stood aside for her to go through the garden door he said: 'You know, you intrigue me.'

'I couldn't care less,' said Polly.

She didn't see him for the rest of that day, nor, for that matter, for the rest of the week. She finished the chapter and started on the next one, completely absorbed in her work, only occasionally bothered by the memory of a dark mocking face.

It was during a morning halfway through her third week there that the maid suddenly burst into the room looking frightened, 'Oh, miss—do come! Sir Ronald's ill—he's lying on the floor in his study and he don't speak!'

'Phone Doctor Makepeace and ask him to come at once.' Polly was already through the door, running across the study to where the old man lay beside his desk.

A stroke, she supposed, loosening his tie and undoing his waistcoat buttons, putting a cushion behind his head and telling Briggs to see that there was someone to have the door open and usher the doctor in the moment he arrived.

After that the rest of the day was a horrible kind of dream, with Sir Ronald carried to his bed, a second doctor coming, followed by a nurse and the entire household at sixes and sevens. Polly abandoned her typing, saw that food and drink were produced at the right times, a room made ready for the nurse and messages sent to Sir Ronald's son and daughter. It was mid-afternoon when the nurse came in search of her.

'Sir Ronald's rallied a little. He wants to see you. Polly, he said.'

'That's me. I'll come.'

Sir Ronald looked very ill and his rather loud voice had shrunk to a thread of sound. 'Get Sam,' he whispered. 'He's to come now. Make him understand. Now. In the phone book—my desk.'

'Very well, Sir Ronald.' Polly's voice was its usual calm self. 'I'll phone now.'

She dialled the number, having no idea where she was dialling. Not a London number, that she did know. And he answered; she would have known his voice anywhere—deep and assured and, just now, businesslike.

'Professor Gervis, this is Polly Talbot. Sir

Ronald told me to phone you. He was taken ill this morning and he wants to see you as soon as possible. Could you come at once?'

She wasn't really surprised when he said: 'I'll be with you in about an hour,' and hung up without having asked a single question.

Polly phoned her home and explained that she would probably be late back, then went away to find the housekeeper and ask her to get a room ready for Professor Gervis. It seemed likely that he would stay the night.

Doctor Makepeace came again presently, bringing his colleague with him. They spent a long time with their patient and then disappeared into the smaller of the sitting rooms and talked. Polly, watching Briggs taking in a tray of coffee, decided that she would wait in the hall and ask just how ill Sir Ronald was. There was an air of gloom over the whole house, with the servants creeping about with long faces, and Doctor Makepeace, whom she had known since she was a child, had looked very solemn. She was sitting in one of the uncomfortable chairs ranged against the wall facing the sitting room when the front door was opened and Professor Gervis walked in. He hadn't rung the bell like any other caller would have done and she hadn't heard his car, although she had been so deep in thought that she might have been deaf to its engine. He wasted no time on the niceties of greeting.

'Tell me what you know,' he said as soon as his eyes lighted on her. He flung a case and a motor coat on to a chair and came to stand in front of her.

She did so in a quiet voice, giving him facts unembellished by guesses or rumours. He nodded when she had finished. 'Doctor Makepeace is here now, you say?'

'Yes,' she nodded to the door opposite. 'In there with the other doctor who came this morning. I was waiting to see Doctor Makepeace . . .'

'Shouldn't you have gone home some time ago?'

'Yes, but how could I? You're staying the night? I asked the housekeeper to get a room ready for you . . .'

'Very thoughtful of you.' He turned abruptly, crossed the hall, tapped on the sitting room door and went inside.

All three men came out five minutes later, but it was Polly waiting that caused Doctor Makepeace to detach himself from the others and cross the hall to speak to her.

'It's good of you to stay, Polly. Will you come into the dining room? I believe Briggs is bringing coffee and sandwiches for us. Professor Gervis wants to talk to you.'

She went with him, wondering why the Professor couldn't have told her himself, or was he as arrogant as he looked?

The two men were standing by the fireplace where someone had lighted a log fire against the chill of the evening. They looked at her without speaking, although the other doctor nodded pleasantly when Doctor Makepeace introduced them, adding: 'Of course, I don't need to make you known to each other, do I?'

A remark which called forth an uninterested glance from the Professor.

She poured the coffee when it came and presently the doctors went away back to their patient. As they left the room the Professor asked: 'What is your telephone number?'

She told him and then added: 'Why do you want to know?' But he didn't answer her, only went to the telephone on a side table and dialled the number. She listened with some indignation as he explained who he was and added: 'I'll drive Polly back within the hour; there are certain matters to be discussed,' and then in answer to the voice at the other end, 'He's very ill indeed. The doctors are with him now.'

Polly, for something to do, poured herself another cup of coffee. Not for the world would she let him see that his high-handed treatment irked her severely. She settled her gaze on an elaborate family group framed in gilt and ignored him.

'And now you'll give me your full attention,' he commanded, 'and be good enough not to interrupt until I've finished.'

She gave him a speaking look and took another sip of coffee.

He had sat down opposite to her so that she had to look at him if she looked anywhere at all. He looked older, she decided, staring rather defiantly at him, and tired, but as ill-humoured as usual. He stared back at her for a long moment.

'Sir Ronald is dying, you must know that. He'll not live the night through. He was quite lucid when I spoke to him just now, and I have given my word that his book shall be published on the date he intended and that you will continue to get it ready for the publishers. That means that you will continue to come here until the funeral, and after that the only possible solution is for you to return with me to my house and complete your work there.' And as she opened her mouth to make a strong protest: 'I asked you not to interrupt. I've had a lot to do with his book and you'll need guidance and someone to check your work. I think that whatever our personal feelings are, we should ignore them and do him this service. It has been years of work and research, and I for one don't intend them to be wasted.' He added with a faint sneer: 'My sister lives with me, which will, I imagine, settle any qualms a girl such as you is bound to have.'

He sat back, one long leg crossed over the other, entirely at his ease. Waiting for her to say yes, thought Polly.

'I'll think about it and let you know tomorrow morning.' Her voice was pleasant enough, but it had an icy edge to it.

'Now,' the Professor's voice was very quiet; it was also compelling. She looked down at her hands, resting quietly in her lap and tried to marshal a few sensible arguments against his wishes. Before she had time to think of a single one the door opened and Doctor Makepeace came in.

'Sam, will you come?' They left the room together, leaving her alone with her thoughts. If Sir Ronald died she would have to accept the Professor's suggestions. The old man had been kind to her after his fashion and she knew without being told that his book had been his greatest interest. She sat quietly, and presently the Professor and both doctors came in together.

'Sir Ronald died a few minutes ago, Polly,' Doctor Makepeace told her kindly. 'A peaceful end, I'm glad to say; a pity he won't see his book published, but I understand that you and Sam are going to carry out his plans. I'll give you a lift home, child.'

'I'll take her back,' said the Professor. 'I'll have

to explain how matters stand to Mr Talbot. It's rather late now, but I daresay we can arrange a meeting tomorrow.'

Doctor Makepeace bustled to the door. 'Good, I've still got a couple of calls to make and I know that Doctor West here wants to get back as soon as possible. You've got the certificates, haven't you, Sam? I'll see you in the morning. When will his son and daughter get here?'

'Tomorrow, I should suppose. Goodnight, and thanks.'

The men shook hands and Doctor Makepeace said: 'He was a good friend to me . . .'

'And to me,' said the Professor, and just for a moment Polly considered that he looked quite human.

'We'll go now,' he said. 'My car's outside.'

'I've got my bike.'

He looked at her without expression. 'You'll be fetched in the morning,' was all he said, and he hurried her out into the hall, where she collected her cardigan, said goodnight to a hovering Briggs and went through the door he was holding open for her. It was dark by now, but lights from the windows showed her a Bentley Corniche parked on the sweep. He indicated that she should get into the front seat and got in beside her. They were almost in the village when he asked: 'Where now?'

'Across the square, up that lane on the other side. The house is on the left, almost at the top of the hill.'

The gate was never shut. He swept past it on to the gravelled sweep before the house and stopped before the door. Polly had hopped out almost before he'd switched off the engine and gone to open it. But it was opened as she reached it and

her father came through it. 'Polly, my dear—
you're so very late, and how is Sir Ronald?' He
peered past her at Professor Gervis looming out of
the dark. 'Someone has brought you home,' he
said, stating the obvious.

'Professor Gervis—my father,' said Polly, very
polite, and then: 'Father, the Professor wants to
talk to you. It's too late now . . .'

'Nonsense, child, we've only just finished
supper. Come in, Professor Gervis, you must meet
my wife and then we can discuss whatever it is . . .'

They were in the dining room, the whole family,
sitting round the table with the remains of a
macaroni cheese and one of Mrs Talbot's fruit
tarts.

Everyone spoke at once until Mr Talbot said
hush and introduced the Professor. 'You were in
church,' said Mrs Talbot instantly, and then:
'You'd like some supper? Coffee?' She put an arm
round Polly. 'You look pinched, darling. Is Sir
Ronald very ill?'

'He died this evening,' said the Professor quietly.
'Polly has been most helpful. I should think she
needs her supper and a chance to talk.' He smiled
across the table at her, looking quite different;
kind and friendly . . .

'I'm sorry. We all liked him. I'll get some coffee
at least, while you're talking. Sit down, Polly, you
shall have your supper. Cora, Marian, get a tray
ready will you?'

Neither of them needed a second bidding. They
rolled expressive eyes at Polly and flew into the
kitchen, and a reluctant Ben having been sent to
bed, Polly and her mother sat down together.
'Now tell me all about it,' demanded Mrs Talbot.
'We guessed Sir Ronald was very poorly the first

time you phoned. Poor man! I'm glad you were able to help.' She cut a generous slice of tart and put it on Polly's plate. 'Why does this Professor want to talk to your father?'

'Well, began Polly, 'it's like this . . .' She explained carefully and then waited to see what her mother would say.

'A very sensible idea,' commented that lady. 'Professor what's-his-name seems to know what he's going to do.' She added reassuringly, 'And his sister lives with him. More tart, love? He's quite youngish, isn't he? Early thirties, I should think. Easy to get on with?' Her voice was casual.

'No,' said Polly forthrightly. 'We don't like each other, but I do see that it's important to get the book published, and I don't have to see him often, you know. Just show him each chapter as it's done, just as I've been doing with Sir Ronald.'

'And where does he live, darling?'

'I don't know.' Polly filled her mouth with tart. 'It can't be very far away,' she said in a crumby voice, 'because he said on the phone he'd be about an hour, and he was—rather less, I think.'

Her mother started to clear the table. 'Well, darling, you've had a rotten day, now you're going straight to bed. There's plenty of hot water and I'll put a bottle in your bed.'

'Oughtn't I to say goodnight?' asked Polly.

'I don't see that it matters,' observed Mrs Talbot cheerfully, 'if you don't like each other . . .'

CHAPTER TWO

PROFESSOR Gervis fetched Polly the next morning, coldly polite and nothing else. He didn't mention Sir Ronald, merely drove her to the house, deposited her at the door, rang the bell and stalked back to his car. She didn't see him for the rest of the day, although Briggs brought her coffee, while she worked and her usual lunch tray. The house was quiet, and determinedly putting everything out of her head other than her work, she typed steadily. At five o'clock she put the completed pages on the desk in the study and went home.

Two more days went by in the same manner, although Sir Ronald's daughter and son were in the house now. But they made no attempt to see her, and save for Briggs she spoke to no one. And the next day was the funeral.

Her mother and father would go, of course, but even if she had had any idea of going herself, they were scotched by the note left on her desk.

'Be good enough to remain here after your day's work. I wish to speak to you.' It was signed S.G.

Polly read it well twice, tore it into little pieces and put them tidily in the waste paper basket, and when it was five o'clock and there was no sign of him, she covered her typewriter and strolled into the garden.

There had been a good deal of coming and going during the day, but the garden was quiet; cars had been leaving for the last hour or so and she supposed the last one had gone. She sat quietly

27

in the last of the sun, deliberately shutting out speculations as to her future. She had promised she would finish the book, so she would do that, but only because Sir Ronald had wanted it so badly. There was nothing about the Professor, she decided, that would encourage her to do anything for him at all.

He came round the corner of the house, unhurriedly, just as though, she thought indignantly, she had the entire evening to waste waiting for him.

'I've kept you waiting.' There was no hint of apology in his voice. 'Is the chapter finished?'

'No.'

He sat down beside her, sitting sideways so that he could watch her.

'Am I rushing you if I suggest that you might be ready to leave tomorrow morning?'

'Yes—you've told me almost nothing, Professor Gervis. Where do you live? How long am I to be at your house, how am I to get there . . .?'

'I live at Elmley Castle, a few miles from Evesham. You will be at my house until the typescript is finished, and I shall drive you there.' He added in a patient voice which made her grit her teeth: 'When you are ready to go, of course.'

'Thank you. Will you be here tomorrow?' And when he nodded: 'I'll let you know then. Of course you want to get back to your own home.'

'Naturally.' He drove her back without another word and to her surprise got out of the car when they arrived. 'I should like to speak to your father,' he explained with the cool politeness she had come to expect when he wasn't being tiresomely arrogant.

She took him along to her father's study and

repaired to the kitchen. Her sisters were out, but Ben was at the table doing his homework and her mother was making rhubarb jam. She looked round as Polly went in and smiled. 'There you are, darling. You're late. Did I hear a car?'

Polly cut a slice of the cake left on the old-fashioned dresser. 'Professor Gervis brought me back. He wanted to see Father. He wants me to go back with him tomorrow, but of course I can't.'

'Why not, dear?' Her mother turned a thoughtful gaze upon her. 'He's anxious to get this book finished, isn't he? I suppose he's got something to do with publishing?'

'I haven't the faintest idea.' Polly stuffed the last of the cake into her mouth. 'He seems to know a lot about it. He's a Professor—perhaps he's a schoolteacher.'

'I daresay, darling. We'll see, shall we? There's not much you have to do, is there? It wouldn't take a moment to pack a bag . . .' Her mother still looked thoughtful. 'They'd better have coffee, hadn't they? Be a darling and put the cups on a tray, will you?'

Polly carried the coffee in presently, to be met by her father's cheerful: 'We're just talking about you, Polly. Professor Gervis is kind enough to say that he won't leave until tomorrow afternoon; that should give you all the time in the world to pack a few clothes and so on.'

She put the tray down on the table beside her father and didn't look at the Professor. 'And what about collecting the manuscript, sorting it out and so on?'

Her father beamed at her. 'Professor Gervis will fetch you tomorrow morning and you can go through the papers together.' He took a sip of the

coffee she had handed him. 'So you see, everything
is very nicely arranged.'

Polly let her mouth open to protest and caught
the Professor's chilly eye. 'The sooner the
manuscript is typed the sooner you will be home
again,' he pointed out with the unnecessary
forbearance of a grown-up cajoling a small child.

She asked woodenly: 'What time will you be
here in the morning, Professor?'

'Ten o'clock. I imagine we can do all that's
necessary in an hour. I'll bring you back, and
perhaps we might leave at three o'clock?'

'Very well.' She gave her puzzled father a smile
and went back to the kitchen.

Presently, his visitor gone, her father joined her.
'A very good man, Professor Gervis. How very
fortunate that he's so enthusiastic about getting Sir
Ronald's book published. He seems to think
you may be finished in a month—perhaps a little
sooner. He suggests that you might like to come
home for your weekends; I thought it very civil of
him.'

'Yes, Father,' said Polly, and went away to look
through her clothes, leaving him to enquire of his
wife if there was anything the matter. Mrs Talbot
returned his questioning look with a limpid one of
her own.

'Why do you ask, dear?' She wanted to know.
'It seems to me to be an ideal arrangement.' She
added: 'Polly's talents mustn't be wasted.'

Polly in her bedroom was packing a suitcase
with a regrettable lack of care. She was thoroughly
put out; she had been got at and in a most unfair
way. She promised herself that she would work all
hours and get the manuscript finished just as soon
as she possibly could; she would take care to see as

little as possible of the Professor, and once her work was finished she would never set eyes on him again. She was dwelling on this prospect at some length when her two sisters, all agog, came tearing into the room, firing questions at her, making plans to come and visit her so that they might see more of Professor Gervis and finally unpacking her case and repacking it carefully with everything properly folded, several of her older dresses flung out, and the addition of her one and only evening dress; a rather plain pleated affair, it's cream background patterned with bronze leaves.

And when she had protested: 'You never know,' declared Cora cryptically. They had wrenched her blouse and skirt from her too, declaring they weren't fit to be seen and guaranteeing that she should have them both back looking like new by the afternoon, so that she had to wear a rather elderly jersey dress in the morning which the Professor studied with obvious dislike. Polly wished him good morning, with her normal calm, got into a Land Rover beside him and was whisked up to Wells Court, with barely a word passing between them, only, once there, she was surprised to find how helpful he was. He had already looked out all the reference books she was likely to need, all that she was left to do was check the manuscript itself and make sure that there was none of it missing. She tied it neatly into its folder, collected the paper and carbon and eraser and would have taken the typewriter too if he hadn't told her to leave it where it was. 'There's the same model at my house,' he told her. 'We've enough clutter as it is. If you've finished Briggs shall bring coffee; I must go and say goodbye to

Sir Ronald's son and daughter.' He paused at
the door. 'Do you know them? Would you like
to meet them?'

She shook her head. 'No, thank you. There's
really no need, is there?' And when he had gone
and Briggs had brought the coffee she sat down
and drank it. Sir Ronald had been a well liked
figure in the village; his children, when they were
home, had never bothered to get to know any of
its inhabitants. Polly hardly thought they would be
interested in meeting a mere schoolmaster's
daughter.

The Professor returned much more quickly than
she had expected. He swept her out to the Land
Rover with a breezy: 'Good, that's done,' and
greatly to her surprise, accepted her mother's offer
of a cup of coffee without hesitation, despite her
discouraging: 'Thanks, I'll see you at three
o'clock,' as he had stopped outside her home. She
excused herself at once, saying that she had to
wash her hair, an operation she dawdled over until
she heard the Land Rover being driven away.

Her sisters had been as good as their word; the
blue pleated skirt looked as good as new, her
cardigan had been washed and pressed to
perfection and there was a small pile of blouses
with a little note begging her to borrow what she
wanted, ending with the hope that she would find
time to buy some new clothes. She smiled as she
packed them; Cora and Marian, both so fashion-
conscious, had never understood why she hadn't
bothered much with clothes. She supposed it was
because she had felt she would be quite unable to
compete. To please them she would take them
both shopping and allow them to advise her as to
a completely new wardrobe. Rather a waste, for

no one would notice her, but at least they wouldn't look at her like the Professor had done that morning . . .

After lunch she changed into a jersey two-piece, a little old for her but suitable for a typist, she considered. And she combed her mousy hair smooth so that it fell on either side of her face almost to her shoulders. This done, she studied her reflection in the pier-glass in her room; it gave her no satisfaction at all, nor did her father's remark that she looked very neat do anything to improve her ego, although her mother bolstered it up again by declaring that her make-up was just right and hadn't she lost weight in the last week or so?

As for the Professor when he arrived to pick her up, his cool eyes travelled over her person without interest.

She got into the Bentley, wondering what he'd done with the Range Rover, and turned to wave at her mother and father and Shylock. She'd be back for a weekend in no time at all; just the same, she felt forlorn at leaving them and to hide it enquired which way they would be going.

'Cross-country to Cirencester and then up the A435 to Cheltenham, then turn off at Eckington. It's not far. Do you know the road?'

'As far as Cheltenham.'

'We could take the Evesham road, but the other way is prettier.'

And after that they lapsed into silence. Polly, feverishly trying to think of something to talk about, was profoundly thankful that their journey was a fairly short one and in the Bentley no more than a forty-minute drive.

The village of Elmley Castle was a delightful surprise; there was no castle standing, of course,

but the village, with its wide main street bordered
by a brook along its length, had a wealth of black
and white cottages and old-fashioned walled
gardens. The Professor went slowly across the
square, past the Tudor inn and turned into a
narrow walled lane, and then turned again
between high brick pillars into the grounds of a
fair-sized house—black and white, like its smaller
village neighbours, with a tiled roof and small
windows, and surrounded by a mass of flower
beds, packed with spring flowers.

'Oh, how very nice,' exclaimed Polly. 'Is this
your house?' And when he nodded: 'And such a
delightful garden—there must be hundreds of
bulbs . . .'

'Hundreds,' he agreed in a voice which
effectively squashed her chatter, and leaned to
open her door.

The house door was open and by the time Polly
had got out of the car a girl not much older than
herself was coming towards them.

Polly hadn't given much thought to the
Professor's sister. She had supposed her to be his
female counterpart—tall, commanding blue eyes
which could turn frosty in seconds, and given to
looking down a softened version of his high-
bridged nose. This girl didn't fit the bill at all. She
was no taller than Polly, with curly brown hair
and large dark eyes, moreover her nose was short
and straight above a smiling mouth. Polly, taken
by surprise, had nothing to say other than a polite
murmur as they were introduced. 'Diana,' said the
Professor laconically, 'this is Polly, who's doing
the typing.'

Polly had her hand taken while Diana said
eagerly: 'I was expecting an elderly terror with

false teeth and a flat chest! How super that it's you. I'll have someone to talk to.'

'No, you won't,' observed her brother severely. 'Polly's here to get that book finished as soon as possible.'

He led the way indoors, but Diana hung back a little. 'He sounds awful, doesn't he?' she wanted to know, 'but he's not really. Of course you'll get time off—you can't type all day.'

Polly thought that was exactly what she would be doing if the Professor had his way, but she smiled at her companion. 'At any rate, my teeth are my own,' she declared cheerfully.

'And you are by no means flat-chested,' observed the Professor from the doorway. 'Come inside, do.'

It was rather dim inside, a good thing since Polly was rather red in the face. She went past the Professor without looking at him and gazed around her. She liked what she saw; a square hall with flagstones underfoot covered with fine rugs, plaster walls above oak panelling, a splendidly carved serpentine table against one wall and facing it a small walnut settee covered with needlework. There were flowers on the table and above it a mirror in a gilded frame with candle branches.

'Where's Bessy?' asked the Professor, leading the way through a solid looking door into a long low-ceilinged room.

'Bringing tea—we heard you coming. Shall Polly see her room first?'

He shrugged. 'Just as you like.' And as a middle-aged woman came into the room with a laden tray: 'Hullo, Bessy, will you give the keys to Jeff and tell him to take Miss Talbot's case up to her room?' He tossed a bunch of keys at her.

'Thank you.' And then: 'Sit down, Polly. This is Bessy, who is our housekeeper and has been for years; I don't know what we would do without her. Jeff is her husband. Don't hesitate to ask them for anything you want.'

He sat down in a large winged chair by the log fire and Diana poured their tea. Polly, always ready to think the worst of him, was surprised when he got up and handed the cups round and followed them with the plate of sandwiches. There was nothing, she conceded, wrong with his manners.

The room was lovely. She glanced around her, as casually as she knew how, to admire the comfortable chairs and huge sofas, little piecrust tables and the glass-fronted cabinets against the walls. There were windows at either end; small leaded, and framed by soft velvet curtains, echoing the chair covers in old rose, and a thick white carpet on the floor which would, she considered, be one person's job to keep clean, especially when there was a scratching at the door and the Professor got up to let in a bull terrier and an Old English Sheepdog, who instantly hurled themselves at him with every sign of delight. He looked at her over their heads.

'Toby and Mustard,' he told her. 'They won't worry you, and they're both mild animals.'

Polly gave him an indignant look. 'I like dogs,' she told him, 'and I'm not nervous of them.'

She offered a balled fist for them to inspect and patted them in turn, and Diana said: 'Oh, good. They roam all over the house, I'm afraid. There are two cats too, do you like them?'

'Yes. We have three at home, and a dog.'

She might not like the Professor but she had to admit that he was a good host; he kept the conversation going without effort and so kindly that she began to feel quite at home, and presently Diana took her upstairs to her room.

The staircase was at the back of the hall, dividing to either side from a small landing halfway up. Diana took the left-hand wing and went down a narrow passage at its head. 'You're here—nice and quiet. There's a bathroom next door.' She flung open a white-painted door and stood aside for Polly to go in. The room was of a comfortable size, furnished prettily in mahogany and chintz, its narrow windows with ruffled muslin curtains. The bathroom leading from it was small but perfect. Polly, eyeing its luxurious fittings said carefully: 'This is charming—I didn't think ... that is, I expected ...'

Diana gave her a wide smile. 'You've no idea how glad I am to have you here. Sam's away all day most days and it's a bit lonely. But I'll be getting married soon ... I'm only staying here because Bob, my fiancé, doesn't like me to be living on my own while he's away.'

'I do have to work all day,' said Polly doubtfully. 'Professor Gervis wants the book finished just as soon as I can get it typed.'

'You must be awfully clever. I never got further than *"Amo, amas, amat"* at school. Sam says your knowledge of the dead languages is extraordinary'. Diana giggled engagingly. 'He said it was an awful waste!'

Polly smiled back at her companion. So it was a waste, was it? But a waste he was quite prepared to put to his own use. 'I'll unpack, shall I? Then perhaps the Professor will show me where I'm to work and I can get everything ready to start in the morning.'

O.K. You are keen, aren't you? Have you got a job? I mean, something else to do besides typing this book?'

Polly shook her head. 'No, but I think I'll look for something when I go home again.'

She thought about that while she unpacked. There wasn't much that she could do. She couldn't bear the thought of teaching, she didn't know enough about clothes and fashion to work in a shop, her arithmetic was poor, so an office job or something in a bank was out. She decided not to worry about it for the moment, arranged her few possessions around the room, and went downstairs.

The Professor was standing at the open front door, his hands in his pockets. Even from his back he looked very impatient.

'I'll show you where you can work,' he told Polly without preamble. 'Jeff has taken everything there and you can start when you like. I shall be out this evening, but you'll dine with Diana at eight o'clock. Perhaps you'll keep office hours while you're here. I'm away for most of the day; but if you'll put whatever work you've done each day on the desk in my study I shall be glad.'

They had gone to the back to the end of the hall and through a small door into a rather bare little room, furnished with a desk and a chair, several filing cabinets and a row of shelves filled with books. There was a typewriter on the desk and the manuscript and paper were arranged beside it. Not a moment to be lost, thought Polly.

'The household accounts and so on are dealt with here,' he told her briefly, 'but no one will disturb you while you're working.' He nodded briskly. 'I shall see you tomorrow evening if not before.'

Polly blinked her preposterous eyelashes at him. 'You'd like me to start now?' she asked, so meekly that he turned to look at her.

'Why not? You're paid for that, aren't you?'

The answer to that piece of rudeness scorched her tongue, but she managed not to give it, instead she went to the desk and started to arrange it to her liking. He watched her in silence until she had put paper in the typewriter and sat down to cast an eye over the manuscript. She was typing the first line when he went away.

'Arrogant idler!' declared Polly loudly to the closed door, and gave a squeak of dismay as it opened and the Professor put his handsome head round it.

'I shall be driving down to Wells Court at the weekend,' he told her, poker-faced. 'If you can bear with my company, I'll give you a lift.'

He had gone again before she could say a word, and she started to type. He couldn't have heard her, or he would have had something to say about it.

She worked without pause until Jeff came to tell her that dinner would be in half an hour, and would she join Miss Diana in the drawing room. 'And I was to tell you, miss, not to mind and change your dress, because there'll be no one but yourself and Miss Diana.'

So Polly went to her room and tidied herself, then went downstairs where she found Diana curled up on one of the sofas, surrounded by glossy magazines. She looked up as Polly went in and told her to get herself a drink from the side table, then come and help her choose something to wear. 'A christening,' she explained, 'and Sam and I will have to go; we're vaguely related to the baby, and Sam's a great one for family ties and all that kind of thing.' She handed Polly *Harpers*. 'That grey outfit's rather nice, isn't it? I'll have to have a hat, of course . . . I don't want to spend too much . . .'

A remark which struck Polly dumb, since the outfit concerned was priced at a couple of hundred pounds. Presently she managed a polite: 'It looks charming, and grey's a useful colour.'

'Useful?' queried Diana, looking surprised. 'Is it? Anyway, I'll nip up to town and have a look at it, I think. I haven't any money, so Sam will have to give me some. I haven't a rag to my back.'

Polly finished her sherry and ventured: 'I expect you go out quite a lot.'

'Oh, lord, yes. It gets boring, some of the dinner parties are so stuffy, and Deirdre—that's Sam's fiancée—has the most tiresome parents. She's tiresome too. I can't think how Sam can put up with her.'

'He doesn't have to,' observed Polly, 'but I expect if he loves her he doesn't notice.'

'Of course he doesn't love her—they sort of slid into it, if you know what I mean, and I suppose he thinks she'll change when they are married. She's very suitable, of course, and they make a handsome pair.' Diana bounced off the sofa. 'Let's have dinner—I'm starving!'

Polly, accustomed to cottage pie and fruit tart eaten in the bosom of her rather noisy family, thought dinner was quite something. The dining room for a start was a dignified apartment, with a large oval table in its centre, straight-backed chairs with tapestry seats, and a vast sideboard. The meal itself, served on white damask with quantities of silver and cut glass, was mouthwatering, far better than the birthday dinners each member of the family enjoyed at one of the hotels in Pulchester. And since Diana had a good appetite, Polly, who was hungry, enjoyed every mouthful of it.

They went back to the drawing-room afterwards to have their coffee, and Diana plunged into the serious matter of clothes once more, until Polly said regretfully: 'The Professor wants the work I've done to be put on his desk each evening; I'd better do that, if you'd tell me which room . . .?'

'Just across the hall, the middle door. Do you really have to go? I'll see you at breakfast, then. Let Bessy know if you want anything.' Diana beamed at Polly. 'Goodnight—it is nice having company, you know.'

Polly said goodnight and then remembered to ask at what time she should come down to breakfast. 'Or do I have it somewhere else?'

'Whatever for? Oh, I see, you start work early, I suppose. I don't get down before nine o'clock. Could you start work and have it with me then? What time do you want to get up? I'll tell someone to call you.'

Polly said half past seven; that would give her time to dress at leisure and perhaps go into the garden for ten minutes before putting in almost an hour's work. 'I said that I'd work office hours', she explained, 'that's eight hours a day. Professor Gervis is very anxious for the book to be finished.'

'Well, don't let him browbeat you. It sounds like slavery to me.'

A very luxurious slavery, thought Polly, getting ready for bed, turning on the shaded lights, sinking her bare feet in the thick pile of the carpet. There were even books on the bedside table. She inspected them eagerly; a catholic selection to suit all tastes. She pottered happily into the bathroom and lay in a haze of steam, wondering what it would be like to live in such a house and eat a dinner like she had just had every night of the week. Probably very boring. No, not boring, she amended; if the Professor was around life would never be boring. She turned on the hot water tap again and began to think about his fianceé. Diana didn't like her, but Diana was a good deal younger than the professor and their tastes might not match. Probably she was exactly right for him and would know just how to run a house such as this one, wear all the right clothes and make intelligent conversation about his work when he got home. As to what he did exactly, Polly was vague and uncaring. Something to do with publishing, she supposed; she pictured him in a plushy office, sitting behind a vast desk, pressing little buttons and summoning people. And that reminded her that she hadn't taken her work to the study downstairs. In a panic she got out to dry herself on an enormous fluffy towel which she had no time to admire, got into her nightgown and dressing gown and went back downstairs. The drawing room door was shut, and there was no sound anywhere. She crossed the hall to her little workroom, collected up the sheets and went back into the hall. The middle door, Diana had said. Polly opened it carefully and shot inside.

The Professor was sitting at his desk, writing. 'Oh, lord,' said Polly, 'I didn't know you were here.'

'So I should imagine.' He had got to his feet and

was looking her up and down, a smile just lifting
the corners of his firm mouth. She didn't much
like the smile; she must look a fright, scarlet from
too hot a bath, hair hanging around her face in a
damp tangle, her dressing gown, a bulky garment
of candlewick, flung on anyhow and tied bunchily
around her small waist.

'I forgot,' said Polly, 'you said you wanted to
see what I'd done each morning, and if I'd waited
till then I might have disturbed you.'

'And what are you doing now?' he enquired
blandly.

'Ah, but I didn't know you were here.' She
thumped the neatly typed sheets down on the desk,
and quite forgetting to say goodnight, nipped
smartly through the door and raced back to her
room. Not a very good beginning, she admonished
her reflection as she brushed her hair.

She was called by a cheerful maid carrying a
tray of tea and a little plate of biscuits, and since
she would have to wait for her breakfast, she made
no bones about draining the teapot and finishing
off the biscuits. She had slept dreamlessly, and
since the sun was shining she got out of bed to
take a look at the day. It was going to be a lovely
May morning; just for a moment she longed to be
at home, free to go out into the garden before
helping to get breakfast. But there was no reason
why she shouldn't go outside now if she dressed
quickly. She was ready in fifteen minutes, very
neat in her blouse and skirt, her hair silky smooth,
her face made up in a limited fashion. Surely no
one would grudge her ten minutes in the garden?

She went softly through the house and found
the front door open, although there was no one to
see, and after a moment's hesitation she turned

along the path running round the side of the
house. It led to a broad expanse of lawn,
circumvented by another path and bordered by
flower beds. She went all round and then took
another path leading invitingly into a shrubbery.
She was nicely into it when she heard dogs barking
and a moment later the Professor's voice. She had
forgotten Toby and Mustard—having a morning
stroll with their master, she supposed. Guiltily she
popped back the way she had come and peered
round her. The Professor was some way off
walking away from her, the dogs bounding ahead
of him. It took only a minute to hurry back to the
house and in through its door. A moment later she
was seated at her desk, putting the first sheet of
paper into the typewriter. She had no need to feel
guilty, she told herself crossly; she was quite
entitled to a breath of air ... She was halfway
down the page when she heard sounds, muffled by
the thickness of the doors, which suggested that
both the Professor and his dogs were back
indoors, and a few minutes later she heard a car
drive up to the house and after the briefest of
pauses drive away again. The Professor had gone
to wherever he went each day. 'And good luck to
him', said Polly loudly, still cross.

She worked steadily until she heard the stable
clock strike the hour, and not before time, for she
was famished and longing for her breakfast. She
found Diana already at the table, reading her
letters, but she put them aside as soon as she saw
Polly.

'Good morning, Polly. I suppose you've been up
for hours—you and Sam should get on well
together—early risers and gluttons for work!
Come and sit down. There's porridge, or grapefruit

and egg and bacon, or Bessy'll do you some kippers if you'd rather . . .'

Polly settled happily for porridge and bacon and egg and listened cheerfully to her companion's plans for the day. 'Such a pity you have to work,' she declared, 'otherwise you could have come with me to Evesham, but I'll be back for lunch.' She pouted prettily. 'I've got to go out this evening, though; Sam says I must. Deirdre's parents are giving a dinner party.' She poured herself another cup of coffee. 'When he marries her I've made up my mind I'll leave here, even if Bob isn't back.'

'Will he be away for long?' asked Polly, which was another way of finding out when the Professor was going to get married.

'Well, he thought three months, but there's always the chance that it'll be sooner than that, and Deirdre's got some stupid idea about being married on Midsummer's Day, although nothing is settled yet. I can't think what Sam sees in her.'

'Well,' began Polly, 'he must see something in her or he wouldn't want to get married . . .'

'Knowing Deirdre, I wouldn't be surprised if she hadn't settled the whole thing without him realising, although he did say she would be very suitable.' She grinned suddenly. 'I'm not at all suitable for Bob, but that really doesn't make any difference, you know.'

Polly didn't know, but she nodded in an understanding sort of way and said regretfully that she would have to go back to her desk.

She worked for the rest of the morning, had lunch with Diana and then went back again to her typewriter. If she kept at it for the rest of the day, she decided, she would be able to put the rest of the chapter on the Professor's desk before she went to bed. She might even get the next one started, since she would have the house to herself that evening.

Diana came looking for her around teatime. 'You really must stop,' she declared. 'You've been working all day . . . come and have tea.'

Polly went willingly enough; she was an active girl and she longed to take a long walk outside while the sun was still shining. 'Well, that's why I'm here,' she explained reasonably. 'Professor Gervis wants the book done just as quickly as possible.'

She allowed herself half an hour and despite Diana's grumbles went back once more to the typewriter. There was still a good bit to do and she was having at present to stop and look things up quite frequently; all the same, she had every intention of finishing the chapter before she went to bed. Deep in a learned comparison between Roman and Greek gods and goddesses, she didn't hear the door open and Diana come in. At the girl's gentle: 'hullo, how do I look?' she glanced up, and instantly forgot these beings in an admiring contemplation of Diana, dressed for the evening. She really was a very pretty girl, and the softly pleated gauzy skirt and tiny beaded bodice merely served to make her doubly so.

'Oh, very nice,' said Polly, and meant it. 'You look a dream. Do you always dress up when you go out in the evening?'

Diana looked surprised. 'Well, yes—especially when Deirdre's going to be there—she thinks she's high fashion personified, you know, so I simply have to outdo her.' She added unnecessarily: 'You like it?'

'It's so beautiful I can't think of a word for it!'

'Don't you like clothes?'

Polly nodded. 'Oh, yes, but you see I'm at home all day, mostly, and I don't need anything like that. I have one evening dress,' she added.

Diana blinked. 'Did you bring it with you?'

She thought for a minute. 'I've got it with me, yes. I wasn't going to pack it, but my sisters put it in.' She added simply: 'You see, I didn't expect to have my meals with you and the Professor.'

'Why ever not?' Diana looked as though she would have liked to have pursued the subject, but a glance at the clock on the austere mantelshelf stopped her. 'Look at the time—Sam'll be shouting for me! Bessy will tell you when dinner's ready—there's a good film on T.V. if you want to watch it afterwards. In the little room at the back of the hall. Sam won't have it in the drawing room.' She whizzed to the door. 'See you at breakfast.'

Polly wasted a few minutes wishing she were in Diana's shoes—and her dress, for that matter—and then went back to the gods and goddesses. She had to concentrate on them so that she barely noticed the faint sounds in the hall or the sound of a car being driven off. She was on the last page when Bessy came in to warn her that dinner would be in ten minutes and the drinks tray was in the drawing room if she would like something first.

At home they drank sherry on birthdays and at Christmas and when there were guests for dinner. Polly went to her room, did her face and brushed her soft cloud of hair, then went back to sip her drink in the grandeur of the drawing room and then to eat her solitary dinner. It was a splendid meal—soup and fried whitebait and lamb chops arranged artistically around a mound of creamed potato and asparagus to go with them. Polly drank the wine Jeff poured for her and finished off with little pancakes, smothered in cream. Tomorrow, she promised herself, she would go for a good walk or she would get fat. She drank her coffee at the table, wished Jeff goodnight and then went back to her work.

It was striking half past nine when she typed the last few words, and she yawned hugely. She hadn't finished, though—first she had to read the whole thing through to check for mistakes; she didn't think she'd made any, but if she had, she was sure the Professor's eagle eye would light on them. It took more than an hour, and she yawned again as she shuffled the sheets tidily together, clipped them and took them to the study. Too late to start the next chapter, she decided, but she would put everything ready so she could make an early start in the morning. She went out of the study and closed the door at the same time as the front door was opened, and Diana, the Professor and another girl came in.

Polly finished closing the door, noticing that the Professor was frowning. In a temper again, she supposed, and wished them good evening in a soothing voice.

'Why aren't you in bed?' demanded Professor Gervis.

'I wanted to finish the chapter. It's on your desk, Professor Gervis.' She smiled at Diana, who grinned back at her, and took a look at the other girl. Deirdre, without a doubt. Tall and dark and willowy—no, skinny, with a horsy face and beautifully arranged hair. Wearing a dress which Polly thought did nothing for her; girls with flat chests and bony arms shouldn't wear slinky sheaths, however elegant they were.

It was Diana who spoke. 'Hullo, Polly, still nose to the grindstone? I hope you took time off for dinner?'

'Oh, yes, thanks. Well, I'll go to bed. Goodnight.' She included all three of them in a wide smile and turned to go.

'Er—just a moment, Polly. This is Deirdre Gordon, my fiancée. Deirdre, Polly Talbot is typing the book Sir Ronald had just completed.'

Deirdre gave her a cold look. 'Hullo. How boring for you.'

'Not a bit of it,' said Polly cheerfully. 'I'm rather enjoying it.'

Deirdre glanced around at her surroundings. 'I expect all this makes a change.' Her rather precise voice held a sneer.

'Well,' said Polly slowly and with great sweetness, 'it's like working in an office, you know, and they're all alike wherever you are. Goodnight.'

She crossed the hall unhurriedly and went upstairs, her head erect, very aware of her workaday skirt and blouse and her untidy head.

In her room she kicked off her shoes and went to run a bath. 'He deserves every inch of her,' she told her reflection, noting with regret that her hair was even worse than she had imagined and her nose shone.

She took a long time getting ready for bed, and once there, picked up a book from the night table, sure that she would never sleep at once. She did, of course, the book slipping from her nerveless hands within five minutes.

CHAPTER THREE

POLLY, much refreshed by a sound night's sleep and tea and biscuits, was at her desk by eight o'clock the next morning. She would work for half an hour or more, she had decided, and then go out into the garden or even stroll down the lane at the end of the drive. Luckily the next chapter was a comparison between Greek and Roman weights and measures and money, something she had studied with her father during the winter evenings. She was well away when the door opened and the Professor walked in. She paused in her typing, put a finger on the page to mark where she was and said good morning.

His own 'good morning' was without warmth. He looked put out, she thought, as he stalked across the little room and planted himself in front of the desk, obscuring her view with the size of him. 'I asked you to type Sir Ronald's manuscript as quickly as possible; I didn't say you were to make a slave of yourself in doing so.' He made a kind of growling noise which she took to be indicative of his annoyance. 'I distinctly remember suggesting nine till five o'clock, but here you are at barely eight o'clock in the morning with your nose on the typewriter!' His voice had a nasty edge to it. 'And another thing—what in the name of heaven do you mean by working until all hours at night? Padding around my house in that deplorable garment, and last night . .'

He paused, glaring down his splendid nose at

her, but before he could speak again: 'Candlewick is awfully bulky,' explained Polly chattily. 'If I'd thought I was going to bump into you, or anyone, I'd have borrowed one of Cora's dressing gowns. And last night,' she went on in a reasonable voice, 'it was something to do—I'd seen the film on T.V. and I didn't like to take a book without asking you. I should have liked to have taken the dogs for a walk, but I don't suppose you'd have liked that. I always take Shylock out in the evenings . . .'

'Shylock?' asked the Professor, almost unwillingly.

'He likes his pound of flesh. And I start work now because I have breakfast with Diana at nine o'clock, which evens things up.' She smiled kindly at him. 'So you have no need to be annoyed.'

He was still frowning. 'Did you go out at all yesterday?'

'Well, no. I was going to ask you, do you mind if I go into the garden sometimes?'

'You may do so whenever you wish, Polly, and it would be a good idea if you took some time off for a walk during the day—or you can use one of the bikes in the shed by the garage.'

'Oh, good!' She smiled at him once more, and he added as though the words were being wrung out of him:

'I hope you'll be happy while you are here.'

She looked surprised. 'I can't think why not.' She added matter-of-factly: 'It's a job, isn't it? And I can go home each weekend—besides, it won't last all that while.' She gave him a friendly nod. 'Now I'm going to get on, and I expect you've got things to do too . . .'

The Professor said nothing; the expression on his face was blandly polite, but his eyes gleamed.

Polly, her neat head already bent over Sir Ronald's spiky writing, didn't see that.

Over breakfast Diana gave her an account of the dinner party.

'It was foul,' she observed succinctly. 'Deirdre's mother and father are the utter end, they call Sam "dear boy" and I can almost hear him snarling when they do—I can't think why he puts up with it!'

'If he loves Deirdre I suppose he'd put up with anything,' said Polly.

Diana turned her large eyes on to Polly. 'Never in this world would Sam be pushed into anything, but the thing is, he's getting on, you know, and I daresay he thinks it's time he settled down and had a family, and since he hasn't found his dream girl I suppose he'll settle for anyone suitable.'

'How very coldblooded,' said Polly severely, 'and he must have met heaps of girls.'

'Of course he has, but none of them lasted. I just wish the right one would come along', Diana sighed as she buttered toast. 'He'd make a good husband—he's a super brother.'

Polly murmured in a noncommittal fashion. She had her reservations about that, but she could hardly say so.

Presently she went back to the little room and buried herself in Sir Ronald's rolling periods.

Diana would be out for lunch. She popped her head round the door after an hour or so, remarked that coffee was on its way and would Polly like to have lunch at the usual time. 'And I'll be back for tea—we'll have it together.'

She was gone, leaving an impression of an elegant outfit, delicious scent and perfect make-up behind her. Polly sat idle for a few minutes; when she had finished this job, she would really buy a super outfit, have her hair done and get Cora or Marian to show her how to make up properly. And hard on these resolutions came a faint idea that she was no longer willing to stay at home, waiting for authors to ask her to type their manuscripts. She wanted to do something— something useful; meet other people, fill her days ... It wasn't that she didn't love her home any more; it was a deep-down feeling of restlessness. She dismissed it for the moment; time enough to make plans when she had finished her work on Sir Ronald's book.

After lunch she went into the garden and found it was a great deal larger than she had thought it to be. At the back of the house the formal flower beds and lawns melted into a partly wild garden which in its turn joined a small copse, reached by a bridge over a narrow stream and a rustic gate. Polly was charmed; it was exactly the kind of garden she liked most, and on her way back, still exploring, she discovered a good-sized swimming pool tucked away behind a beech hedge. Not yet in use, she guessed, although there was a charming little hut beside it, used for changing, she supposed. It would be heaven to swim in the early mornings in the summer and then go back to the house and eat one of Bessy's magnificent breakfasts.

She got a good deal of work done before Diana returned home, and once they had had tea, she went back to her desk, despite Diana's protests. The chapter was a long one and she intended having at least half of it done, ready for the Professor to check in the morning.

All the same, mindful of his remarks earlier that

day, she put the cover on the typewriter as the clock struck six and went up to her room. She was uncertain what to wear, but she certainly couldn't go down to dinner in a blouse and skirt. She showered and got into a brushed cotton dress, an off-the-peg model from a multiple store and, despite its cheapness, pretty. And then, since it was still barely seven o'clock, she slipped on a cardigan and went quietly downstairs and out into the garden.

It was a beautiful evening, but cool. She walked through the wilder end and crossed the bridge and went into the copse. It was very quiet there; she stood still and listened to the birds and then wandered on. The Professor was lucky to have such peace so near his home, although probably he had neither the time nor the inclination to enjoy it.

She was mistaken. Halfway along the path, well and truly into the trees, Mustard and Toby came tearing towards her, barking wildly, and strolling behind them, the Professor.

He stopped in front of her with a polite: 'Good evening, Polly,' then turned about to walk beside her. 'Pleasant after a hard day's work, isn't it?' he observed blandly, and Polly, not sure if he meant a hard day's work for her or for him, agreed.

'I see you're getting on well with the typing,' he remarked. 'Let me see, how many more chapters have we to do?'

She rather took exception to the 'we', but since he was disposed to be so friendly she said merely: 'Six, and the glossary.'

'Which will take considerably longer than a chapter. Three weeks' work, do you suppose?'

'I'll do my best—perhaps I can do it in less.'

'Naturally you want to get finished as quickly as possible. Have you any plans for the future?'

He asked the question in so casual a manner that she answered at once. 'No—at least, I intend to do something, but I'm not sure what.'

They had reached a fork in the path and he took her arm for a moment and guided her to the left. 'There's a small stream at the end,' he explained. 'We can walk along the bank and return down the other side.'

The stream was clear and shallow and fast-flowing, and as they stood by it they could hear the gentle plop! as the water-rats and voles slipped into it from their holes. 'There's a kingfisher here,' observed the Professor quietly, 'but you have to come early in the morning to see it.' He glanced down at her intent face. 'We should be getting back, I think.'

Dinner was a pleasant meal with conversation which gave Polly no clue as to the Professor's life or work. True, Deirdre was mentioned once or twice, but in such general terms that she learned nothing more than she already knew. It was at the end of the meal, as they were crossing the hall to the drawing room to have their coffee, that the Professor said: 'I have to go to Wells Court this weekend, Polly. I'll give you a lift. Would early, and I mean early—Saturday morning—suit you? I had intended going down on Friday evening, but I'd forgotten that Deirdre had asked me to take her to see some friends.'

'Well, thank you, that would be super. What time is early?'

'Seven o'clock, before breakfast.'

'Oh, well, yes—that's fine.' She drank her coffee and got to her feet. 'I'll say goodnight. I usually go to bed quite early.'

He opened the door for her. 'Of course I'll bring you back on Sunday evening,' he told her as she went past him.

She didn't see him again until quite late on Friday afternoon, driving up to the house just as she was gathering together the last of another chapter. She waited a few minutes until she heard him go upstairs, followed by the dogs, then she went along to the study, laid the sheets on his desk and went back again to the little room she now considered hers. There was time to glance through the next chapter, the eras of Greek and Roman literature, and set everything for Monday morning. It was going to be a long one, starting well before 400 B.C. and then, under headings, ending at around 150 A.D. It was stuffed with names, too, which would slow her down at typing. And there were four more chapters after that one. She resolved to work a little longer each day. The Professor was anxious for her to finish. She was perhaps tiresome to have in the house, even though he was away all day, and besides, she told herself firmly, she wanted to be finished too—as quickly as possible. It was almost eight o'clock by the time she had read all she wanted; she would have barely ten minutes in which to shower and change her dress. She raced upstairs, to bump into Professor Gervis coming down, very elegant in his dinner jacket. She paused just long enough to say: 'I'm late—so sorry, I was reading . . . the rest of the chapter's on your desk.'

He put out a long arm and caught her lightly. 'I did say that you were to work from nine to five o'clock?' he queried gently.

'Yes—yes, you did, and I do mostly.' She

smiled at him. 'I hope you have a pleasant evening.'

He let her go. 'I hope so too,' he muttered.

She was in the hall on the stroke of seven o'clock the next morning but he was there before her. And at her quick: 'I'm late . . .' reassured her with: 'No, I took the dogs for a run.'

It was a bright May morning and Polly, in a jersey shirtwaister, not high fashion but suiting her well enough, settled back into the luxury of the Bentley. The Professor, she could see, was disposed to be friendly, and somehow in a sweater and slacks he looked quite approachable. They talked when they felt like it in an easy fashion, and it wasn't until they were in the front of her house that Polly realised that he hadn't said one word about himself. She wasn't by nature a curious girl, but now she felt the strongest urge to discover as much as possible about him—perhaps it was that which prompted her to invite him in for breakfast. 'But only if you want to,' she added carefully.

'There's nothing I should like better,' he told her, then stood quietly by when the door opened and Polly flung herself at her mother.

The whole family sat round the table, all talking at once while they ate the bacon and eggs and toast and marmalade which Mrs Talbot produced. They drank the enormous teapot dry too, and Polly, remembering the elegant silver coffee pot on the breakfast table and the calm of the Professor's house, wondered if he was really enjoying himself as much as he appeared to be. Certainly he was making himself quite at home, and once the meal was finished, he went off to Mr Talbot's study to look at some book or other they had been discussing. Polly, drying cups and saucers, expressed her surprise to her mother. 'You'd think he'd want to get to Wells Court as soon as possible,' she said in a puzzled voice.

Mrs Talbot said, 'Um', thoughtfully, then asked: 'He mentioned his fiancée—why isn't she here too?'

'I've no idea—perhaps it was a bit early in the morning.'

Mrs Talbot rinsed a plate carefully. 'Time doesn't matter when you're in love, darling.'

'Yes, but Deirdre—his fiancée—isn't like that, Mother. She's quite perfect, and far too thin. I don't like her.'

'Well, no, my dear, I hardly expect you to.' An obscure remark which Polly only half heard, for the Professor and her father were in the hall and a moment later in the kitchen.

'I'll fetch you about half past seven on Sunday evening, Polly,' said the Professor. He spoke pleasantly, but he sounded, and looked remote.

No sooner had he gone than Cora and Marian rushed at her. 'Lucky you, even if he is going to get married! You're coming into Pulchester now, this minute, and you're going to buy some clothes. That thing you're wearing is at least two years old. Have you got any money?'

Polly said yes, she had, and prudently halved the amount, adding that while she was perfectly willing to buy some clothes, they were to be the kind she could wear every day, and how were they to get to Pulchester anyway?

Cora's current boy-friend had a car; by lunchtime Polly had spent all the money she had allowed herself and under her sisters' critical eyes had bought a cotton skirt and blouse in a pleasing shade of pink, a sleeveless dress in cream jersey with a knitted jacket in all colours of the rainbow and a pair of rather frivolous sandals, not at all her usual kind. Her sisters exchanged glances and said nothing, nor did they question her wish to buy a dressing gown, on the plea that the candlewick was too warm. They encouraged her to choose a flimsy trifle the colour of apricots and pooled what they had in their purses to get her matching slippers. Undoubtedly little Polly had woken up to the fact that pretty clothes did make a difference, especially if she was wanting to attract attention to herself. They plied her with discreet questions on their way home, and were disappointed to hear that she rarely saw the Professor and that when she did, they almost always fell out over something or other. 'That's why,' Polly assured them earnestly, 'I'm trying to get finished just as quickly as I can. It's lovely being there—I mean, the house is heavenly, and my bedroom is out of this world and the food is super, and I like Diana, but Professor Gervis will be glad when I've gone, I'm sure. He looks at me as though I oughtn't to be there, if you know what I mean.'

Her sisters exchanged another look and began to question her closely about Deirdre. They did it so well that Polly answered all their questions readily enough, even repeating what the horrid creature had said when they had been introduced.

'Not his type at all,' observed Cora thoughtfully. 'I wonder how he got caught?'

'Caught? You can't catch someone like the Professor,' declared Polly.

'The cleverest of men are quite often fools,' said Marian.

It was Sunday evening far too soon. Polly

packed her new clothes, took Shylock for a long walk after tea, then sat down to wait for the Professor. He arrived exactly at seven o'clock, spent five minutes in a friendly desultory talk with her family, all of whom he found at home, ushered her into the Bentley, and drove off. Polly waved until they reached the corner and then sat back.

'You enjoyed your weekend?' he wanted to know.

'Oh, yes. Did you enjoy yours?'

'I had some things to clear up for Sir Ronald.'

'Oh, I'm sorry; you couldn't have had much fun, then.'

'And what do you mean by fun, Polly?' he asked pleasantly, so that she was emboldened to explain:

'Well, being happy, taking the dogs out or riding or pottering round talking to people, or just sitting with the Sunday papers.'

'All on my own?'

She looked at him in some surprise. 'But there were people there . . .'

'Sometimes I would rather be on my own.'

'I expect you miss your fiancée. She's very— very . . .' Polly paused, seeking the right word.

'She is acknowledged as the local belle—a word I use for want of a more modern one.'

'Well, you must be very proud of her.' She turned to smile at him and met a blank stare which had the effect of putting her immediately in her place, and if that wasn't enough, he began to question her about her work. They talked about that, off and on, for the rest of the drive.

It was quite a relief to find Diana waiting for them when they arrived, ready to talk for the three of them.

At dinner she told her brother that Deirdre had

telephoned that morning. 'She wants to see you—
she didn't say why, but she sounded cross.'

'In that case I'd better go over and see what it's
all about.' There was nothing in his face to show
annoyance, but Polly had the idea that he was
angry. None of her business, she warned herself,
spent half an hour with Diana and went to bed.

She was up early and since it was a lovely
morning she went out into the garden, carefully
going in the other direction to the dogs bark. She
was making her way, circumspectly, to the house
when she heard the car drive off.

She didn't see the Professor for four days. Each
evening she laid the work she had done on his
desk, and since he wasn't there, she worked early
and late. By Thursday evening she had two
chapters there and was well into the next one.

She hadn't liked to ask Diana where he was, and
since he wasn't mentioned at all, she had to
contain her curiosity, so she was completely taken
by surprise on Friday morning, when, after a stroll
round the garden, she was deep in a highly
involved chapter concerning the pronunciation of
both Greek and Latin when the door was thrust
open to admit both dogs and the Professor.

He didn't bother with a good morning, which
made Polly's greeting all the more polite.

'You've been working overtime?' he asked
accusingly.

Polly bent to pull gently at the dogs' ears. 'To
please myself,' she told him airily, and wondered
why she was so glad to see him again, seeing that
he hadn't even the good manners to wish her a
good day.

'I expressly . .' he began.

She chipped in before he got going. 'Professor

Gervis, I don't suppose you've considered anyone else other than yourself over this business of getting Sir Ronald's book published. Indeed there's no reason why you should, I suppose. But I should like to point out that I'm as anxious to get it finished as you are. Not because I'm not enjoying the work—I am, very much, but I do have plans which I don't want to delay for too long.' She smiled at him kindly, without effect.

'What sort of plans?'

Polly frowned. How like him to pick on the one weak point in her careful little speech! 'I don't think it's necessary to bother you with them.'

'Not going to tell me, eh? Well, if that's the case, go ahead and work as much as you wish. When will you be finished?'

'In two weeks' time, unless I'm thwarted.'

He gave a great shout of laughter. 'No one would dare!' He whistled to the dogs, lifted a hand in casual salute and went away.

Polly didn't do anything for quite a while. She had said all that about having plans on the spur of the moment, but the idea, once in her head, stuck firmly, crystallising the vague plans she had had to do something useful. She couldn't teach, she would be hopeless in a shop and the idea of sitting at a desk typing all day quite sickened her, which left only one other thing she might be able to do. She could train as a nurse. She pondered over this for a few minutes, and then, satisfied that she had hit on a solution, went back to the Romans and the Greeks once more.

There was a paper shop in the village; there was no sign of the Professor and Diana had gone to friends for lunch. Polly got on to one of the bicycles from the shed behind the garage, and cycled through the narrow lanes to where Mrs Prosser presided over a selection of newspapers, magazines and sweets. She was a nice old lady, and helpful. To Polly's question as to whether she sold a nursing magazine, she said that of course she did; the district nurse collected her *Nursing Times* regularly each week, but there was only her copy. 'There being no call for more,' she pointed out. 'Why?'

Polly explained in a roundabout way; an address of a hospital for a friend, and could she possibly just take a peep at the district nurse's copy?

Mrs Prosser didn't see why not. Polly bought a Mars bar and perched on the only chair in the shop to leaf through the vacancies columns. There were several London hospitals wanting student nurses, but London was too far away and so was Manchester. She was just about to give up when her eye lighted on a Birmingham children's hospital; immediate vacancies, it stated, and gave a phone number to enquire for application forms. Polly made a hasty note of the address, bought another Mars bar, thanked Mrs Prosser and got back on the bike. There was a phone box a little further down the road, and she believed in striking while the iron was hot.

The application form came the next day, she filled it in, hopefully, then went back to Sir Ronald's book.

The next day was a Saturday and she was free to go home should she wish to do so. She phoned her father in the evening, coaxed him into fetching her on Saturday morning, and since Diana and the Professor were out again, spent the evening typing, only stopping for an hour for dinner and a quick walk round the garden with the dogs.

She had warned Diana that she would be going home after breakfast and would she mind if she had it early, and when she went downstairs there was no one about but Bessy, who wished her a cheerful good morning and served her breakfast. Of the Professor there was no sign; Polly took it for granted that he was away from home.

Her father arrived a little early and she lost no time in climbing into the car beside him, explaining that there was no one about and there was no point in waiting round. And on the way home she told him what she had done. Rather to her surprise, he thought it a splendid idea. 'There are so few openings for your particular talents, my dear,' he told her, 'and nursing is a profession which offers great opportunities. You can climb to the top of the tree if you wish—Matron of one of the big hospitals.'

Polly thought privately that she had little desire to be a Matron. She would like to marry and have children, and enough money to bring them up in comfort, provided by a husband who adored her and lavished impossible things like diamond rings and cashmere sweaters and Gucci handbags upon her. She sighed and her father asked: 'Tired, my dear? How is the book going?'

'Two weeks and it'll be finished, Father. If the hospital asks me to go for an interview I thought I'd decide on next Saturday, so I won't be home . . .'

'Nonsense, my dear, you go to Birmingham if they want you to, and give me a ring. I'll fetch you—after all, there'll be a lot to talk over if they consider you.'

There was a lot to talk about when she got home too. The family, a little astonished at the turn of events, all the same gave her their enthusiastic blessing. 'And of course,' her father pointed out, 'your knowledge of Greek and Latin will stand you in good stead, you know—Latin terms are prevalent in medical books.'

So the weekend passed happily enough, with Shylock as a companion on a long walk and church on Sunday and her mother's delicious roast dinner afterwards. She hated leaving them all again. All the same, as her father stopped outside the Professor's impressive porch, she felt a little spiral of excitement. Not excitement, she told herself severely, merely a precautionary bracing against his dislike of her.

She wished her father goodbye, got her overnight bag from the back of the car and with a final wave, tugged the old-fashioned cast-iron bell beside the door, but before its clanging had ceased the door had been flung open and the Professor, with a brief hullo, had passed her, going to the car. Polly turned round to see her father getting out and coming indoors with his host, and slid ahead of them into the hall.

The Professor stopped briefly by her. 'Come down to the drawing room, Polly, we can all have coffee together.' And she nodded. Thank heaven she had warned her father to say nothing of her intention of training as a nurse; she could imagine the curl of the Professor's lip at the very idea.

Diana was there too, and two nice elderly people from the village who seemed to know the Professor and his sister very well. They were charming to Polly, and an hour passed quickly before her father got up to go.

'I'll see you next week, my dear,' he told her as she kissed him goodbye, and only a warning

glance stopped him from saying anything more.
He coughed to cover his confusion, added, 'Yes,
well . . . give me a ring, Polly,' and she sighed with
relief, all of which the Professor noted with
interest.

Now that the weather was settling into warmth
and sunshine, Diana was out a good deal, which
meant that Polly had time to herself. She put in
more hours than she was supposed to, went to the
village from time to time, and got into the habit of
taking the dogs for a run as far as the little stream
through the wood. There had been a reply to her
application; she was summoned for an interview
and, most luckily, the following Saturday was one
of the days suggested. She wrote off at once and
then spent most of the next night lying awake
wondering if she had done the right thing. Too late
now, she told herself, and sensibly went to sleep,
albeit for a mere couple of hours.

Of the Professor there was no sign, although she
was almost sure that he came home at night and
went very early in the morning, and although by
now she was on very good terms with Diana, she
couldn't bring herself to ask about him. She
finished the chapter and began on the next; a nice
easy one, mostly concerned with Sir Ronald's own
opinions concerning the previous chapters. Two
days, she reckoned, and then only the final one
and the glossary.

It was after tea on Thursday, and she heard the
Bentley whispering up the drive and then the
Professor's voice in the hall. She went on typing,
one small corner of her head deciding to wear the
sleeveless jersey dress. She had worn the pink
separates and Diana had admired them, but a
change would be nice.

She finished the work she had decided to do, despite a desire to go to her room and get changed for the evening, and finally gathered together the finished sheets, left her desk tidy, and took her work along to his study. She hesitated before she knocked, then jumped nervously as he called from the stairs: 'No, I'm not there—go in and leave the papers on my desk, will you?'

She gave him a brief glance, nodded and did as he asked. When she came into the hall, he had gone.

Not even a good evening, she mused, going upstairs, it's just as though I'm not here.

She took a long time bathing and changing into the new dress, doing her face, brushing her newly washed hair. The result, while not spectacular, was pleasing enough. The dress was nicely cut and showed off her pretty figure, and its deep cream went well with the faint tan she was already getting. She waited until ten minutes before the gong would go, then went downstairs.

Diana was in the drawing room, and so was the Professor; so, too, was Deirdre. Polly stopped just inside the door, arranged her face into a social smile and said: 'Good evening—I didn't know you had guests.'

Deirdre was lolling back on one of the sofas, wearing a blue crêpe trouser suit and a lot of jangling jewellery. She gave a little laugh. 'My dear . . . I've forgotten your name, so sorry . . . I hardly count myself as a guest, and I'm sure that if there'd been guests for dinner Diana would have made arrangements for you.'

'Yes, I would,' said Diana instantly. 'Polly would have been invited.' She shot Deirdre a furious look and then turned her eyes on her brother.

'Oh, most certainly,' declared the Professor smoothly. 'Polly's quite one of the family.' He smiled at her so kindly that her stiff face relaxed into a genuine smile. 'And what will you drink?'

From then on he kept the conversation in his own hands, not giving Deirdre much chance to make any more spiteful remarks, talking about a hundred and one topics with an ease Polly envied. She ate her dinner without having much to say for herself, although she answered politely when she was spoken to, conscious that the jersey dress was totally inadequate when seen in the company of pale blue crêpe and Diana's simple and expensive silk dress. The prospect of another hour or so in Deirdre's company after dinner was not to be borne. After coffee in the drawing room, Polly made her excuses in a composed voice, wished everyone goodnight, and went from the room. It was comforting that the Professor, holding the door for her, uttered a soft, 'Goodnight, Polly,' of his own as she went past him, but the evening, as far as she was concerned, had been quite awful. She went upstairs and stood looking out of the window, knowing that the mere sight of Deirdre had so annoyed her that she wouldn't sleep if she went to bed.

'So silly,' said Polly to the moon, already climbing the early summer sky, 'to let her upset me—after all, I'll never see any of them again once I leave here.' She found the thought so upsetting that she determined on action.

She could reach her little office by way of the back stairs and a narrow passage on the ground floor. She would go down and read through the work she intended to do in the morning; it saved time in the actual typing if she checked spelling and punctuation and references first.

It was cool in the little room. She went and switched on the reading lamp on the desk, left the door ajar, then sat down to read. She had been there for half an hour or so when she heard voices and footsteps coming in her direction. She switched out the lamp and sat like a mouse, praying that whoever it was wouldn't stay in the hall. But they did; the Professor and his Deirdre, obviously having a leisurely chat before she left the house. To close the door would have been the right thing to do, but one or other of them might see that, and she could just imagine their faces if they found her sitting there in the dark. She went hot at the very idea. She would, of course, put her fingers in her ears. She was on the point of performing this laudable act when she heard her own name, uttered by Deirdre.

'Such a suitable name—Polly. She's a nonentity, poor girl—no looks and so dull, and that awful dress! Where does she buy her clothes, I wonder?'

'I've no idea.' The Professor's voice was coolly uninterested. 'She looked rather nice this evening, I thought, and you're mistaken as to her dullness, Deirdre. She has more brains in her little finger than you have in the whole of your pretty head.'

Deirdre gave a titter. 'You're always so forbearing, Sam—I daresay it's because you don't care about such people.'

He sounded bored. 'Probably. I think you're being unnecessarily unkind.'

'Darling Sam, if I wasn't sure that you were my devoted slave I might think you were angry!' And when he didn't answer: 'Oh, well, what a boring talk we're having, aren't we? Are you going to be at the Bradshaws' on Saturday? We'll see each other there, then. I've bought the most divine dress—wait till you see it!'

They were walking away towards the door of the house. Polly heard the sound of a car door slamming and goodnights being called. She wouldn't be able to go yet, but the Professor would go back to the drawing room and she could slip upstairs. She sat quietly staring out into the darkened garden, fighting a strong wish to cry. And that would be silly, she told herself fiercely, just because a spiteful girl had vented her spite . . .

The door opened wide and the Professor stood framed in the doorway. He didn't put on the light. 'I'm sorry you had to hear, Polly,' he said in such a gentle voice that her throat was choked with the tears she had been fighting.

Presently she managed! 'How did you know?'

'Deirdre uses Chanel Number Five; you're wearing something quite different, light and flowery.'

'Oh, I do hope she didn't notice too. I didn't mean to listen, only I couldn't very well come out, could I? Your fiancée would have felt awkward . . .'

'Deirdre never feels awkward,' he said drily. 'I'm sorry, Polly. Deirdre hasn't met anyone like you before,' he went on carefully. 'She lives such a different life from yours she finds it difficult . . .'

'Don't apologise, Professor.' Polly had got her usual calm voice back again. 'It really is of no importance. Oh, I was a bit upset, but not any more. Probably I shan't see her again, and one forgets these things.'

'You're a very nice person, Polly. I for one find you . . '

She interrupted him: 'I know—brainy, but still dull and badly dressed.' She got to her feet quickly and whisked past him and ran upstairs to her room.

She was down at her usual time in the morning, relieved to have heard the Bentley being driven away while she was still dressing. She would only have to see him that evening at dinner, and the next day was Saturday.

She walked round the garden, wishing she could have spent an hour there, for the fine weather had brought on a multitude of flowers, but it was more important than ever to get the book finished at the earliest possible moment. She had made good headway by breakfast time and the whole day stretched before her. She returned Diana's good morning cheerfully and even managed to laugh at that young lady's opinion of her future sister-in-law. 'She's the utter end,' said Diana, 'she bores me to tears; all she can talk about is herself and clothes. Well, I like clothes too, but not all day and every day. Sam will go spare once they're married. She's still on about the romance of being married on Midsummer's Day, but I heard Sam say he didn't think he could fit it in.' She gave a delighted chuckle. 'Can you imagine a man, really in love, not being able to fit in his wedding!' She nodded her head darkly. 'I'm just waiting for the crunch. There's going to be one, you know.'

Polly finished her coffee. 'Well, I shan't be here to know about it. Perhaps Deirdre will be nicer once she's married.'

'You must be joking, Polly! There's nothing nice about her. I suppose you're going to work? Oh, well, at least I'll see you at lunch, won't I?'

That was a pleasant interlude in the day's work for Polly, although she didn't loiter over it. She had planned to finish the chapter and she did. What was more, she began on the last one of the book.

The Professor didn't come home, and she told herself she was glad. It would make going in the morning easier, for she would have to go down to the village and catch a bus for the first part of her journey to Birmingham. If he were home, he would probably want to know why and where she was going, but Diana wasn't a curious-minded girl. Polly told her as they went to bed that she was going early in the morning and would be back on Sunday evening, and beyond expressing regret that Polly wouldn't be there to talk to, Diana made no other comment.

Polly, more than ever determined to take up her new career as soon as possible, although she wasn't quite sure why, put some things into her overnight bag and got into bed, taking care not to think about the Professor at all.

CHAPTER FOUR

THE hospital was in the heart of the city, gloomy red brick and old-fashioned windows. But Polly wasted no time in inspecting it; she marched firmly in and enquired where she should go.

The porter was friendly. 'Come to see the Chief Nursing Officer?' he asked. 'Go to the back of the hall and turn left—there's a door.'

The door opened on to a kind of waiting room, rather bleak and smelling very faintly of hospitals. There were three other girls there. Polly wished them good morning and received muttered replies, so she sat down composedly and waited. The three girls went in, one after the other, and finally it was her turn. The woman behind the desk was quite young, pleasant and good-looking. Polly, who had always imagined hospital Matrons to be elderly, sharp-featured and critical, changed her ideas at once.

'Why do you want to nurse?' she was asked.

'I'd like to do something useful.'

'I see you're something of a scholar. You have excellent A-levels.'

'No one wants Latin and Greek,' Polly explained. 'I'm typing a book now—it's almost finished—for a scholar. He died a few weeks ago, but I don't suppose there'll be another one for years.'

Her companion looked at her thoughtfully. 'Probably not. You like children?'

'Oh, yes. I haven't done any nursing, though.'

'It's very hard work. Can you give me two references, Miss Talbot?'

Not the Professor, thought Polly rapidly. The Reverend Mr Mortimer and Doctor Makepeace would do nicely. She gave names and addresses and was told that provided her references were satisfactory she might start her training in two weeks' time. 'Instructions will be sent to you before then, and you will have to have a medical examination. There's a three months' probationary period, and if you wish to leave before then, you will be free to do so.'

Polly, waiting for her father outside New Street Station, had a great deal to think about. She would have to work flat out in order to get finished in a week; that would give her a week at home. Of course, she could work over the next weekend and leave in the early part of the week. She went to the station buffet and had a cup of coffee and did little sums all over the back of an empty envelope. She had quite a lot of money and she would get a salary at the end of the month. All of a sudden she felt gloriously independent.

There was a great deal of talk at home too once she got there. Her parents were pleased, although her mother looked despondent too. 'You won't be seeing that nice Professor again, I suppose,' she said hopefully.

'Well, no, Mother. Why should I? I'll have finished in a week's time, and it was only a temporary job.' She spoke casually, her mind on other things. 'I don't suppose I'll come home every week,' she reflected. 'We get two days off, but I'll have to get to know Birmingham and do shopping and things like that. You could come and see me . . .'

'Yes, love, but you'll make friends, you know. We're going to miss you.' Her mother sighed soundlessly. 'I'd hoped that Professor Gervis might have found you a job—I mean, if he's in the publishing business he must know lots of people.'

'I daresay he does. But why should he, Mother? It was just convenient that I should finish the book. I daresay he knows dozens of people who could have done it far better than I have.'

Her father drove her back on Sunday evening, and this time, because there were lights streaming from the drawing room windows and the sound of voices, he drove off at once, leaving Polly to ring the bell and when Jeff opened the door, go inside. It was an awkward time to return; she had had a good tea at home, but now it was half past eight and there were obviously guests in the house. It looked as though she might get nothing to eat. And she was suddenly famished.

'There's folk for dinner, miss,' offered Jeff. 'Shall I bring you a tray of something presently?'

'Oh, Jeff would you? I'll come down to my work room, shall I? Sandwiches would do . . .'

'If you'll come to the small sitting room in ten minutes or so, there'll be something for you there.'

Polly skipped upstairs. There was quite a volume of sound coming from the drawing room; the Professor was entertaining on a large scale. She unpacked her bag, tidied herself and went obediently to the small sitting room. Not small at all, in actual fact, only compared with the drawing room.

There was a small round table near the window and on it Jeff had arranged a cloth, plates and cutlery. Without comment he served her with soup, lobster patties, roast lamb and one of

Bessy's mouthwatering trifles. Halfway through her meal, watching Jeff arrange the new potatoes beside the lamb, Polly asked: 'Jeff, is it really all right for me to be here? I mean, you must have heaps to do with the guests.'

He gave her a fatherly look. 'They've already dined, miss. Professor Gervis said that if you were to return too late to have dinner with everyone else you were to be served here.'

Polly blinked. 'Did he? How—how thoughtful of him, and thank you, Jeff. I hope I haven't given you and Bessy extra work.'

'Not at all, miss. I'll bring coffee here, shall I?'

'Please, then I'll go upstairs.'

She was refilling her coffee cup when the Professor came in.

'I heard you come back,' he observed. 'I had hoped you would be here in time for dinner with the rest of us. Still, never mind, you must come and have a drink now.'

'Oh, my goodness, no!' declared Polly, and at his look added apologetically: 'I didn't mean to be rude. It's just that I'm not dressed for parties, and I—I shan't know anyone there.'

'Me? Diana? Deirdre too.' He smiled suddenly: 'No, I can see you would rather not join us.' To her surprise he sat down opposite her at the table. 'Have you had a pleasant weekend?'

She was unaware of the guilty look on her face. She said hurriedly: 'Oh, yes, thank you. I . . . we . . . it's always lovely to go home.'

He was studying her telltale face with half closed eyes. 'And you will be finished by next weekend?' he wanted to know blandly.

'Yes, oh yes—at least, if you wouldn't mind, just to be on the safe side, would it bother you if I stayed until Sunday—that would give me all Saturday to make a final check. The last chapter's very short and the glossary won't have any words in it that I haven't already come across.'

'You've found it interesting work?'

'Yes, very.'

'And you've been reasonably happy here?'

'Oh, yes, indeed I have.'

'Very little to do, I'm afraid. The occasional cycle ride to Mrs Prosser's shop, perhaps?'

Polly went pink. Surely he didn't know about her looking at the *Nursing Times*? He couldn't possibly. She had no way of finding out and it didn't matter anyway. All the same, she squirmed when he went on pleasantly: 'Have you a job in view, Polly?'

'Yes—no, that is, in a way, yes.'

He got up at last. 'For a Greek scholar you're singularly muddled in your speech this evening. Perhaps you're overtired—why not have a few days off and postpone the rest of the typing for a little while. Another week won't make all that difference.'

'Oh, but it will,' cried Polly: she didn't imagine one could write to the hospital authorities and say that one would be a few days late because it wasn't convenient to arrive when told to do so. She was aware of his raised eyebrows and added hastily: 'I mean, it's so much easier to keep on once I've got started if you know what I mean.'

He didn't answer that, only smiled again, wished her goodnight and wandered to the door. 'We shall all miss you here,' he told her. 'Goodnight.'

She worked hard for the next few days and since there was no sign of the Professor, she put the last chapter on his desk and began to type the glossary—a slow, careful job which kept her busy from early morning until late in the evening, although she was careful to have her meals with Diana and allow her to have the impression that she was enjoying a certain amount of leisure too. Once or twice, while she had been working, she heard Deirdre's voice in the house, and once the Professor's deeper tones, but he didn't come near her and it wasn't until Friday evening that she saw him again.

She was in the garden with the dogs, throwing them an old tennis ball and racing round like a little girl when she was brought up short by his: 'Good evening, Polly.'

The dogs rushed at him and he stooped to pat them, looking over their heads at her. 'I'm glad to see you're enjoying yourself. I take it the book is almost finished?'

She was still bewildered at the pleasure she felt at seeing him again. 'Yes, very nearly. You've been away, I expect you're glad to be home again.'

He was still staring at her. 'Yes, very glad, although I daresay I'll change my mind about that presently. I have to go out to dinner this evening and I would so much rather be here.'

She stood awkwardly, wishing to go and yet surprised to find that she was enjoying his company.

'I'll drive you home on Sunday,' he told her. 'I should like a word with your father and I have to go to Wells Court.' And at her uncertain look: 'I really do have to go, so you might just as well have a lift. I'd like to leave about eight o'clock. Will that suit you?'

'Yes, thank you.' She turned on her heel and he turned with her.

'I must go back, I suppose.' He walked with her to the side door and opened it. 'Goodnight, Polly.'

She murmured goodnight and slid past him, to go up to her room, where she sat down on her bed, puzzled as to why she should feel sad at the idea of leaving the Professor's house, when it had been her one aim to get away from it as soon as possible.

She finished the last page on Saturday evening, having worked doggedly throughout the day. The Professor had driven away quite early in the morning and she hadn't seen him since, and after breakfast Diana had gone off to play tennis with friends. She had been apologetic about it. 'It seems a bit mean on your last day, Polly, and I can't think why Sam had to go thundering off so early, but I'll be back after lunch and we're both home for dinner this evening—your last evening . . .'

Polly paused, buttering toast. 'I hope that isn't because of me,' she said matter-of-factly. 'I haven't quite finished, you know, and I'd be quite happy with something on a tray.'

'Nonsense! Besides, we'd like to be at home for once. What are you going to do now you've finished the book?'

'Have a few days at home, and then see what turns up,' said Polly rather cagily. She would have liked to have told Diana about the hospital, but although a dear girl, Diana couldn't keep anything to herself. Polly paled at the idea of the Professor's caustic remarks if he should discover that she was going to train as a nurse. Not that he'd been caustic lately; indeed, thinking about it, she was forced to admit to herself that barring one or two slight differences of opinion, they had become quite friendly.

There was still no one home as she put the last

of her work on the desk in the study and then went upstairs. She would wear the pink separates, she decided; the linen was out of the question after Deirdre's remarks.

Not that it matters what you wear, she told her reflection as she did her face. She heard Diana come into the house presently, and a little later, the Professor, but she didn't go down until there was barely five minutes before dinner, and when she did there was no one in the drawing-room. She sat herself down in one of the easy chairs and picked up a magazine, and presently was rewarded by the sound of someone coming downstairs.

The Professor, and in a hurry. He flung the half open door wide, put his head in and said: 'So sorry I have to go out after all. I'll see you at breakfast.'

Before she could reply he had gone again, to come back a moment later, crossing the room to her with a long stride. 'You look very sweet in that pink dress,' he told her, and while she was still staring at him in surprise kissed her soundly. And this time he didn't come back.

Diana came in presently. 'Sam's gone out—what a life he leads! What luck he wasn't taking Deirdre out—she's away, thank heaven—she grumbles for hours on end if he stands her up.' She wandered over to the drinks set out on the sofa table. 'Sherry? Have you finished? I'm going to miss you, Polly, although I'm more out than in, aren't I? But it passes the time until Bob gets back—only another week.'

'And then you'll get married?'

'Just as soon as we can. I want you to come to the wedding—it'll be here in the village, so you could drive up, couldn't you?'

Polly didn't answer at once. 'I'd love to come, but if I've got a job I might not be free.'

'Then play truant, or whatever you call it, from work. Have you any plans to marry?'

Polly shook her head, aware once more of the puzzling feeling of sadness. She shook it off and said cheerfully: 'None at all. That's a good thing, because either Cora or Marian is sure to get married soon, they've each got a fistful of aspiring husbands.'

Dinner was a happy little meal because both of them did their best to make it so, and afterwards they sat in the drawing-room, watching the long June day fade into a lovely evening and discussing clothes—Diana's in particular. 'I'm going on a shopping spree next week,' she declared happily. 'I'll need masses of new things, I haven't a rag fit to wear.' They sat there until quite late talking and drinking their coffee, until finally Polly declared she would have to go to bed. 'I've still got some packing to do,' she said by way of excuse. 'You don't mind?'

She escaped upstairs, disappointed that she hadn't seen the Professor and at the same time thankful too. He might have thought that she had sat downstairs on purpose, that they might meet again. She thought of his surprising kiss and then dismissed it from her mind. Probably he'd had some good news or something similar which had made him feel happy. More than likely if it had been Bessy instead of herself, he would have kissed her. She sighed deeply for no reason at all, and got into bed.

They met at breakfast. Polly, wishing him good morning in a calm voice, thought that the Professor looked tired; certainly, although he answered her civilly enough, he showed no sign of wanting to talk. It wasn't until Diana joined them that there was any conversation worth mentioning, and that was of a tepid nature. Polly had barely finished her second cup of coffee when she was asked if she was ready to leave. She rose from the table composedly, inwardly put out at the way the Professor was rushing her away, just as though he was glad to see her go. Well, very likely he was, she told herself sensibly as she went to collect her things from her room and then pop down to the kitchen to wish Bessy and Jeff goodbye. Which made her arrive in the hall rather later than she had intended, to find the Professor, a model of contained impatience, sitting on the edge of a console table while Diana, still eating a slice of toast, was curled up in a chair.

'So sorry,' said Polly, 'but I had to say goodbye to Bessy and Jeff and the dogs. I'm ready now.'

The Professor made a sound which could have been a laugh, although she doubted that, and went to the door, to wait while his sister said goodbye. Diana always had a lot to say, it took five minutes for Polly to get into the Bentley beside him and then another two or three because Diana had remembered something she simply had to say to her. They drove off finally in a silence which augured ill for a pleasant journey, but presently he asked, to surprise her: 'Do you think me a bad-tempered man, Polly?'

She wasn't to be hurried into a rash answer: she said after some thought: 'I don't think that you're naturally bad-tempered, only when you're frustrated or disappointed about something—like most people. Of course you don't like to be crossed, do you?'

'That largely depends on who's trying to cross me.' He overtook three cars in succession. 'Diana will miss you, she's been lonely for the last few weeks. It's a pity she and Deirdre don't like each other. And you, Polly, do you like her?'

She thought it prudent to mistake his meaning. 'Diana? I think she's a darling girl . . .'

'Don't prevaricate—I'm talking about Deirdre.'

She surveyed the pitfalls ahead and sighed. 'I don't know her, do I? She's pretty and attractive and—and . . .'

'But you don't like her. She doesn't like you.' His voice was dangerously silky.

'Well, she has no reason to, has she?' observed Polly sensibly. 'We're most unlikely to meet again . . .' She added severely, 'And I can't see any reason for this conversation, Professor Gervis, so may we talk about something else?'

'But I had a reason,' he informed her blandly— and then added lightly: 'You have got something lined up for your future?'

'Yes, thank you,'

'Not going to tell me about it? Being cagey?' He sounded amused.

'I am not cagey . . .'

'And it's none of my business. I can take a hint, like anyone else. Let us discuss the weather.'

Which, most infuriatingly, he did for the rest of their journey.

Polly had supposed he was going to Wells Court when he had dropped her off at her home, but common good manners forced her to ask him if he would like coffee before he did so. His instant and willing agreement quite put her out, although right at the back of her mind was the thought that she would be seeing him for a little while longer. She squashed the idea before she could think about it too deeply and opened the front door on to a wave of Talbots, all eager to rush them indoors.

'We haven't gone to church,' burst out Ben. 'We're going this evening instead—we wanted to be at home when you got here.'

Polly threw an arm round his shoulders. 'How lovely to see you all again—I should have hated coming home to an empty house.' She moved away a little to say hullo to her mother and watched from the corner of her eye the rest of the family bear the Professor off into the drawing room.

'How very kind of Sam to bring you home,' declared her mother as they put cups on a tray for coffee. 'And really you should be with the others—how like your sisters to monopolise him the moment he arrives!'

Sam? thought Polly; she must ask her mother about that later. Now she said placatingly: 'Well, Mother, they're great fun as well as being pretty, and I've only been working for him—we hardly know each other.'

Not quite true; hadn't he kissed her once? But did a kiss like that count in any way? She thought not. He was a disturbing element in her life though and far too bossy; a good thing he would be going in half an hour or so.

In this she was over-optimistic; the Professor, invited to share Sunday lunch, expressed his delight at being asked and accepted. Cora bounced into Polly's room where she was unpacking, to tell her so.

Polly frowned. 'Don't any of you dare to say a word about my going to Birmingham next week— I'll never forgive you!' She was kneeling on the floor putting undies away in a drawer and looked over her shoulder at her sister. 'You haven't said anything, have you? I did ask all of you . . .'

'O.K., Polly, don't get so desperate about it! No one has breathed a word and we won't. Anyway, he hasn't asked any questions—he's been talking about the book with Father and chatting us up— you haven't been mentioned. He's outside now, showing Ben how to drive the Bentley.' She gave a little giggle. 'Oh, if only I'd been a Greek and Latin scholar, I'd have put it to good use, I can tell you!'

'A lot of good it would have done you,' said Polly matter-of-factly. 'He's engaged. She's an absolute horror but very pretty in a thin kind of way, and she wears gorgeous clothes.'

'When are they going to get married?'

'I've no idea, though Deirdre—that's her—told Diana that she thought it would be romantic to get married on Midsummer Day. Of all the silly sentimental nonsense, and she's not romantic either.'

Cora looked thoughtfully at the bowed head of her sister. It wasn't like Polly to get so heated about anyone or anything; she was the most level-headed, goodnatured girl alive, only the strongest of motives would make her really angry.

They went downstairs presently and laid the table before Polly went to the kitchen to help her mother, while Cora slipped away to where the rest of the family were grouped around the Professor in the garden. Presently the group split up and the two girls wandered back into the house, though not at once into the kitchen. Cora pushed Marian smartly into Mr Talbot's tiny study and closed the door gently.

'Whatever's the matter with you?' demanded Marian.

'Nothing—it's our Polly. I'm sure she's head over heels in love with Sam and hasn't the faintest idea.' Cora shook her head. 'She's such a child over that kind of thing—her head's stuffed with Greek verbs and she's not like us—I don't suppose she even thinks about him, not knowingly, because he's supposed to be marrying this twit of a girl on Midsummer Day.'

Marian giggled. 'What an idea! Are they in love—he and this girl, I mean?'

'Shouldn't think so. I mean, if they were, she'd have come too, wouldn't she? From all accounts he's away each and every day, so they can't see much of each other. What shall we do?'

'Nothing, how can we? We're not even sure . . . besides, he doesn't really notice her, does he, or talk about her.'

'No, I'm not sure that that isn't a good sign. We'd better go and mingle in the kitchen or Mother will want to know where we are.'

At the door Cora paused. 'He'd make a lovely husband for Polly.'

Marian nodded. 'She'd present him with a row of handsome little Greek and Latin scholars, all very dark, like Dad.' They laughed softly and then Cora said: 'It's not a joke really. Polly's not like us.'

Sunday lunch at the Talbots' was something of a ritual—roast beef, Yorkshire pudding, roast potatoes, vegetables from the garden and one of Mrs Talbot's fruit pies with lashings of cream. The Professor did full justice to them all, complimenting Mrs Talbot on her cooking so that that lady went quite pink with pleasure.

'Though I daresay you have a cook of your own?' she questioned.

'Yes indeed. Bessy has been with us for such a long time I can hardly remember when she first came. I should be lost without her.'

'You'll find her a treasure when you're married,' observed Mrs Talbot.

'Er—yes.'

'Perhaps your fianceé is a good cook?' ventured Mrs Talbot.

Just for once the Professor was at a loss. 'I really don't know,' he observed, and bore the battery of Talbot eyes turned upon him with commendable sangfroid.

'Oh, well, it's something which comes with practice,' said Mrs Talbot comfortably.

The Professor showed no signs of hurrying away after the meal; he strolled round the garden with his host for half an hour or more before finally bidding all of them goodbye, promising Mr Talbot a copy of Sir Ronald's book when it was published, exchanging the lighthearted badinage with Cora and Marian that they expected, offering beautifully mannered thanks to Mrs Talbot, giving Ben a manly thump on the back and lastly turning to Polly.

'Many thanks for your hard work, Polly,' he uttered the words casually. 'You've done very well—Sir Ronald would have been delighted.'

With which brief speech he got into the car and drove away.

Polly was kept too busy during the next day or two to have time to think about Professor Gervis, and when she did find that her thoughts were dwelling upon him, she made haste to change them rapidly. He was gone, and that was that, and since they had never got on very well, there was no reason why she should bother with him.

He might be gone, but the memory of him was very clear in her head. It was disconcerting to find herself thinking of him the moment she woke in the morning, and thinking of him again far too frequently during the day. Even plunging into the task of getting her things ready to go to hospital didn't prevent her doing that. It was a matter of regret that she hadn't wished him goodbye—true, she had mumbled something, but he'd paid no heed.

It was two days before she was due to leave home and she was out walking Shylock in the early morning, still mulling over their unsatisfactory parting, when she stopped suddenly in her tracks, almost falling over a surprised Shylock. Midsummer Day wasn't all that far off now, and the very idea of the Professor marrying Deirdre on that day made her feel quite ill. Deirdre wasn't the girl for him; she would be a ghastly wife, and he would become more irritable and impatient with every month that passed. He needed someone sensible, who could ignore his arrogance and ill humour, see that he didn't work too hard, and run his home for him—something Deirdre would never do—for Bessy and Jeff, already uneasy when she was in the house, would never be happy once she had gone there to live.

Polly flopped down on a tuft of coarse grass. 'Oh, my dear Sam, it's me you need!' she declared loudly, and then because there was absolutely no way of making that possible, she burst into tears.

It was silly to cry, she told herself ten minutes later, and mopped her sodden face carefully.

Crying for the moon would get her nowhere. Of course, if ever there was a chance . . . She sat and daydreamed for another half an hour, then shook herself into common sense again, and went back home to breakfast, and if her family thought that she was rather quiet, they put it down to last-minute fears at the idea of taking up nursing, although as Cora told Marian, they couldn't be sure of that.

Her father drove her to Birmingham, saw her safely inside the hospital doors, wished her goodbye with the rider that they would see each other again on her days off, and drove away, leaving her in the care of the chief porter, who advised her to take a seat while he rang the office. And after that it was a quick succession of happenings, one after the other, until she found herself at last in her room in the Nurses' Home—a small room, but nicely furnished, and her uniform was laid out on the bed ready for her to put on in the morning. She unpacked, arranged her few bits and pieces on the windowsill and dressing table and, mindful of instructions, locked the door and found her way downstairs.

Tea, the warden had told her, was in the hospital canteen, but since she and half a dozen other girls were just arrived, they could have it in the sitting room on the ground floor.

There were five girls sitting around the large comfortably furnished room, all looking a bit lost and not attempting to pour their tea from the large pot on the tea tray. Polly said, 'Hullo,' and gathered a chorus of replies, and then because it was something to do, advanced to the teapot. 'I'm Polly Talbot, shall I pour for us all?'

It broke the ice nicely. Names were exchanged,

opinions given as to their rooms, the warden, who looked quite nice, and the Nursing Officer who seemed a bit severe. 'It's like going to school for the first time,' declared one girl, pretty and dark with large eyes and a mop of hair. 'I can't think why I ever decided to come!'

Everyone laughed, looking at each other, wondering who would be friends with whom, remembering that they would be seeing a great deal of each other for the next three years. They were really beginning to enjoy themselves when the warden came in to tell them that supper was at eight o'clock and if they wanted to go out before then, they could. Polly, with the plea that she had letters to write, arranged to meet the other girls in the hall just before eight o'clock, and went back to her room. She was suddenly and profoundly unhappy. Though she was certain she had done the right thing, and that after a time life would be fun again, just now there was no fun at all. She had done her best not to think about Professor Gervis, but not very successfully so far; he lived inside her head, his voice was in her ears and the time she had spent at his home unwound itself continuously like a never-ending film. 'And why I had to fall in love with you, my dear,' she admonished the wall, 'I do not know, because we're quite unsuited and you've never even noticed me—well, almost never. Besides you're going to get married.' And the thought of that made her feel even sadder.

They trooped in to supper feeling strange and awkward. The canteen seemed full of nurses, all looking their way, but it was better once someone in an overall had shown them a table where they could sit together. They queued for their supper, ate it in a rather subdued fashion, then left in a body, to crowd into Polly's room and talk. They were a nice lot of girls, she decided, and a good thing, since they were to spend a good deal of time together. 'Who tells us where to go in the morning?' asked someone.

'We'll get told at breakfast, I should imagine,' said Polly, 'Let's make up our caps and see how we're going to look.'

They passed the time happily enough until a rather haughty girl with a different cap from theirs put her head round the door and warned them that lights had to be out by eleven o'clock.

'Who was that?' asked Polly. 'And what a fetching cap.' She was standing in front of the small mirror, turning this way and that, deciding at which angle to wear her own headgear. She had to pin up her hair because the cap looked ridiculous on her straight shoulder-length locks, and she was fairly satisfied with the result. At least she looked older—a good deal plainer too.

There was no point in lying awake worrying about the morning, she allowed herself a few minutes' daydreaming about the Professor and then sensibly went to sleep.

At breakfast, selfconsciously eating cornflakes in her uniform, she was told that she was to go to Beecham Ward. One of the nurses working there would take her—only for the mornings, though; in the afternoons she was to go to the classroom and have lectures from Sister Tutor and she would be free each evening at five o'clock. Polly nodded goodbye to the other girls in her group and followed the hurried footsteps of a tall, thin girl with a face like a friendly horse. 'You'll like it,' she flung over one shoulder as they hurried upstairs along numerous corridors. 'Sister Bates is nice,

Staff's a bit sharp, but don't let it worry you. What's your name?'

'Talbot, Polly Talbot.'

'Like children?'

'Yes—yes, I do.'

'Good.'

They were almost at a double swing door. 'Are you—that is, how long have you been here?' asked Polly.

'Two years. Name's Honeybun, Freda.'

The first thing that struck Polly as they went through the doors was the noise—children shouting and wailing and laughing and crying. 'You'll get used to it,' observed her companion. 'It's when they're quiet that you have to worry.'

She was led to Sister's Office where the girl who had put her head round the door yesterday evening was sitting at the desk. She looked up as Polly was ushered in and then left. 'Hullo. You're Talbot—Polly Talbot, aren't you? Sister will want to see you when she comes on duty. Ever done any nursing before?

'No, only a small brother with measles and mumps and chickenpox.'

'Oh, well, that's something, I suppose. Come along, you can help with breakfasts.'

And that meant gently shovelling food into a two-year-old with a leg in plaster, and then bottle feeding a six-months-old baby, and then a four-year-old had to be helped to eat his porridge between bouts of rage. Polly, having won a limited victory over him, was nonetheless relieved when she was told to go to Sister's Office.

Sister Bates was a small round middle-aged woman with a firm chin and a kind mouth. She cast aside the papers before her on the desk and invited Polly to sit down.

'We're glad to see you, Nurse Talbot—we can always do with an extra pair of hands on the ward. You will be here for three months, for the first month you will spend your afternoons with Sister Tutor, after that you will do normal duties. You will have two days free each week—I make out the off duty two weeks at a time so that you can plan trips home and so on—and you'll be free each day at five o'clock.' She looked up and smiled. 'I daresay you'll be tired, all you'll want to do is climb into your bed. Take my advice and don't. Get out for a walk first.'

She looked at a paper she had picked up from her desk. 'You will work with a second-year nurse and sometimes with Staff Nurse Stockley, sometimes with me. Routine jobs to start with, cots and beds, wiping up messes, washing toddlers, bathing babies, feeding ... fetching and carrying, too. You'll learn a great deal from just looking and you may ask all the questions you want to, but you'll find that your lessons in the Training School tie up with your work.' She smiled again. 'You look a sensible girl. Is there anything you want to know?'

'No, thank you, Sister.'

'Good. Go back to Staff, will you, and ask her to come here, and then work with Nurse Honeybun. When she goes to coffee will you go with her.'

Polly went back into the ward, delivered her message and started making up cots with Freda Honeybun, listening carefully to that young lady's stream of information and advice, and looking around her at the same time. There were twenty cots and small beds in the ward, although it seemed far more than that, on account of the noise. The ward was divided in the centre by a wide arch, there were large barred windows with cheerful curtains. There were miniature tables and chairs too and gay posters pinned on to the walls. Even with the alarming number of rules and regulations her companion was pouring out to her, Polly knew she would like it.

It was true, of course, what Sister Bates had told her; she was dead on her feet by five o'clock. The day had been one continuous round of chores, some of them very unpleasant, all of them necessary, and she had only the vaguest idea as to the various ailments the children suffered from. It was a surgical ward, so there were surgical conditions, but she couldn't see under the bandages and dressings and she probably wouldn't for weeks to come. All the same, the day had brought satisfaction with it and hardly a moment in which to think of the Professor. Despite cries of anguished protest from the other girls in her set, she doggedly got out of uniform, had a shower, dressed again, went out. The hospital was very much in the centre of the city and there wasn't anywhere much to go to, but she found a small park not too far away and walked round it several times before going back to have her supper.

The next three days followed the same pattern, but by now she was finding her feet. She could tell the difference between first and second and third-year nurses, could name most of the Ward Sisters, knew where the Path Lab was and the theatre wing, and no longer looked blank when Staff Nurse Stockley told her to feed the intususception baby. All the same, it was hard going, but she welcomed it; it kept her mind off other things.

On the fourth morning she went on duty feeling

that she was getting the hang of things. It was Theatre day, an important weekly event still to be experienced; it was also round day; whatever that might be, but far more important, she had two free days starting at five o'clock that afternoon. Her father had promised to fetch her, although she would have to wait until the evening, all the same she would be home for supper. She hugged the thought to her as she spoon-fed a toddler with a hare lip, admitted the day before and still to be examined. The houseman had told her that; Joseph Taylor, young and keen and friendly, and not above talking to a junior nurse. The Registrar she had seen from a distance, but he talked only with Sister or Staff Nurse. He was a tall, stooping man, very good at his job, although he tended to ignore the nurses. He was reputed to have a jealous wife, but that could be hearsay.

Polly finished feeding the small girl, tidied the plate away and wiped the little disfigured face clean and then kissed it. She perched the moppet up against the pillows, arranged a teddy bear and a doll on the coverlet and turned to go, a little flustered because the swing doors had opened and she could hear Sister's voice and a number of feet. She would have to go towards them, there was no other way. She took a step and stopped dead in her tracks. Professor Gervis was standing there, smiling a little.

CHAPTER FIVE

QUITE forgetful of where she was and unaware of the shining delight in her face, Polly spoke. 'Great heavens, is this where you work? And I thought you were a publisher! What a surprise . . .' Her eye caught Sister's look of outrage and she went slowly scarlet, then darted past the group of people surrounding the Professor, down the ward and into the sluice room, where she shut the door and leaned against the sink, feeling sick with shame and surprise and horror that she would be instantly dismissed. Surely any minute the doors would be flung open and she would be forced to go back to the ward. But that didn't happen. Through the thick door she could hear voices coming nearer and retreating again, and then only the normal sounds to which her ears had grown accustomed. She had just made up her mind to go back into the ward to face Staff's caustic tongue— not that she minded that so much; just as long as she didn't have to see Professor Gervis again; when the door opened and Nurse Honeybun peered round it.

'You're wanted in Sister's Office,' she said urgently. 'Whatever happened? We were all at this end so we missed it. You'd better be quick!'

Polly went past her into the ward. She still felt sick, but the quicker she got there the sooner she would know what was to happen to her. Sister Tutor, rather on the elderly side and old-fashioned with it, would never forgive her. Hadn't she spent almost one whole afternoon making sure that the class realised that junior nurses—very junior nurses at that—did not address the consultants unless they were delivering a message or giving information, which they had been asked for? 'And if Sister is there, you will give any message to her and she will tell the consultant.' Which made the consultant seem a terrifying being living in a kind of glass case. They had giggled about it among themselves, but now it was no laughing matter. With a silent moan Polly tapped on the door and went in.

Sister wasn't there, but the Professor was sitting at the desk with a pile of notes before him. He looked up as she went in and got to his feet, his firm mouth twitching into a smile, quickly suppressed as she said wildly: 'Oh, don't get up, Sister wants me . . .'

'She sent the message because I asked her to. Sister has gone to have coffee on the Medical Ward. Sit down, Polly.'

She hesitated, all her calm forsaking her. 'I've got a lot to do in the ward—it's time for the feeds—I must . . .'

'Don't twitter, Polly.'

She sat then, and he folded his length back on to Sister's chair.

'You weren't surprised to see me,' she stated. 'How very unfair of you!'

'I'm sorry,' he didn't sound sorry in the least. 'I'm on the Board of Governors here and naturally all applications come to my notice.' His mouth twitched once more. 'I did give you ample opportunity to tell me, Polly—why so secret?'

She looked down at her hands folded tidily on her cotton lap. 'I didn't think you'd be interested.'

She sounded forlorn, but only for a moment. 'I expect you found it very funny,' she went on, suddenly severe, forgetful of all Sister Tutor's teaching. 'I daresay I'll get the sack for being cheeky to a consultant—you are one, aren't you? We're not supposed to talk to them, you know.'

'I know that only applies to on-duty hours, though.'

'I was on duty,' she reminded him sharply.

'Yes, but I explained to Sister that we were old friends and you'd been taken by surprise—she was very nice about it. I see you have two days off. Are you going home this evening?'

'Yes, Father's coming for me.'

He picked up the phone. 'Well, we can save him a journey. I'm going to Wells Court on my way home; I'll drop you off,' and when she snappily refused, he went on blandly: 'My dear girl, it's no trouble, I go past your door.'

Polly sat there, listening to him dialling her home, explaining charmingly to her mother, refusing, apparently with regret, her offer of supper. 'About half past seven, then,' he finished pleasantly, and replaced the receiver.

'I'll be outside the front entrance at six o'clock, will that give you enough time, Polly?' And as she started to get up: 'No, don't go for a minute. How do you like your work here? Not very interesting at the moment, I imagine—feeding and potties and babies being sick and trying to remember how to get to the Dispensary or the Path Lab.'

'I like it very much.' She had regained her cool now, delight at seeing him well damped down. 'Do you come here every day?'

He smiled slowly. 'Yes, most days—I operate

three times a week, and there's an outpatients clinic and a post-op clinic and the ward rounds. I go to Bristol too, I have beds at one of the hospitals there.'

'So why do you publish books as well?'

'I don't. I helped Sir Ronald for several years; I have an interest in Latin and Greek and we had that in common; no one else would have bothered to get his book published, and I happen to be on good terms with the director of a firm which deals with that type of literature. Do you have to screw your hair up like that, Polly?'

She gave him a surprised look. 'Well, I can't wear a cap with my hair hanging round my neck, it wouldn't be allowed, and it doesn't make any difference . . .'

He studied her for a long moment. 'No, it doesn't. You want to go, I expect. Don't let Staff Nurse Stockley bully you—Sister Bates will allow our—er—friendship to filter through the grapevine, so you need not fear to hear any more of this morning's incident.' He stood up as she went to the door. 'You looked pleased to see me,' he observed quietly.

Her hand on the door, Polly turned to look at him. 'I was taken by surprise,' she said with dignity.

Later, sitting beside Nurse Honeybun while they fed two babies, she explained a little: just that she had known Professor Gervis and had been surprised to meet him again. 'That's what Staff told me,' said Honeybun. 'Sister told her and said it was quite natural that you'd been surprised and forgotten your hospital etiquette. She told her she wasn't to say anything to you.' She added with satisfaction, 'Always quick to criticise, is our

Staff.' She cast a sidelong glance at Polly. 'He's nice, isn't he? Stops and talks to us, and plays with the babies and comes in at all hours if there's an emergency.' She held the baby over one shoulder and patted its back while it belched gently. 'Hard luck on his wife, when he gets married—someone said he was engaged. You know that, of course—is she pretty?'

'Yes, very,' said Polly tonelessly. Providentially, the baby she was feeding began to bawl loudly and so there was no more talk.

She was the only one of her set with days off; the others had all had theirs. They walked in and out of her room while she changed and showered and then packed a few things into her overnight bag.

'Going by train?' one of them wanted to know.

Polly was brushing her hair into a silky curtain. 'No. Car.'

'Being fetched, are you?'

'Well, no, not exactly. I'm being given a lift.'

'Lucky you. Anyone we know?'

It was surprising how friendly they had all become in one short week, asking and answering questions about each other, borrowing and lending, copying each other's notes. 'Yes—you may have seen him. It's Professor Gervis.'

There was a chorus of excited voices. 'Polly, how did you manage it? He's a consultant!' The word was uttered with reverence.

'Well, I know his sister and he knows my father. He's got to see someone who lives near us, so he said he'd drop me off.'

'But how did he know you were off duty?'

'I suppose he . . . I've no idea, I didn't think to ask.'

Someone said lightly: 'Well, make hay, Polly . . .'
Everyone laughed.

'He's going to be married quite soon,' Polly told
them. 'I'm off—I'll see you all on Sunday evening.'

The Nurses' Home could be reached from the
street, but there was an underground passage
connecting it to the hospital too. Polly, walking
briskly along it, listened to the sounds which
penetrated even there. Only at night was the
hospital quiet and that quiet was often broken by
a small child's crying, or a baby's wailing, now it
was a cumulative tide of noise, muffled by thick
walls. She had grown used to it during the last few
days.

She took the wrong turning at the end of the
passage and had to retrace her steps so that she
arrived in the entrance hall faintly harassed. And
suppose he wasn't there? Suppose something
important had cropped up, and he'd forgotten to
let her know? Suppose he had been joking? She
went slowly to the great entrance doors and just as
slowly through them.

He was there, sitting in the Bentley, and since
his eyes were closed, very likely asleep. She went
close to the car and since he didn't move, peered in
to jump back with a half-suppressed shriek as he
suddenly opened his eyes. Polly withdrew her
head, half in the window. 'I'm so sorry, I didn't
mean to wake you up . . .'

'I wasn't asleep, just waiting for you.'

She said: 'Oh,' uncertainly, and stepped back as
he got out. He took her bag and slung it on the
back seat and went round to open the door for
her, then got in himself. Even in such a big car, he
overlapped on all sides.

It was a splendid evening and still warm, and

there was a great deal of traffic, but once free of the city, the Professor shot ahead. They didn't talk much at first, but presently he began to tell her about the hospital and his work there, and Polly listened with pleasure. Never before had he offered one grain of information about himself or his work; now he was explaining his long absences from home, the occasional night call, seminars in other countries.

'It sounds so interesting, and it must absorb a great deal of your life,' observed Polly. 'Do you have time to do the things you like—I don't mean your surgery, but your free time . . .'

'I've always found time for anything I want to do. The unimportant social stuff goes largely by the board.'

'Yes, but when you marry you'll want to visit friends and have them back.'

'Naturally, but there's a vast difference between having friends in for a meal and making social conversation with a lot of people I can't stand.'

Polly murmured gently in reply and wondered what Deirdre would have to say to that. Presently she said: 'But you do—did go out a lot. I expect Deirdre has a great many friends.'

It was the Professor's turn to murmur, it was more a murmured mutter and sounded rude. Polly thought it prudent to talk about something else. 'Will you tell me about the children you look after? I don't think I'll ever learn enough to be a good nurse.'

It was mortifying when he agreed affably, but he went on to tell her about one or two of the more interesting cases in his care, and she listened carefully, although it was his voice she was listening to more than his words.

As they slowed down the hill with home in sight, she wished the journey could have taken longer. Probably she wouldn't see him again for days. At least, she supposed he would come on to the ward, but he wouldn't speak to her and she certainly wouldn't speak to him. It would be sensible to go right away where she would never see him again, but she couldn't bear the fearful thought of that.

He turned into the short drive and pulled up before the door, and Mrs Talbot came out so smartly that she must have been lying in wait.

'I know you can't stay for supper,' she said at once, 'but you simply must have a cup of coffee—it'll only take five minutes to drink.' She offered a cheek to Polly and smiled at him.

'I'd like to, Mrs Talbot, but only for five minutes—I'm due to go out this evening.'

They went indoors and the coffee was fetched while he and Mr Talbot chatted briefly. Cora and Marian were out and so was Ben, and the house seemed very quiet, and true to his word, the Professor was on his feet again the moment he had finished his coffee. Not surprising really, thought Polly, with the girls not there to amuse him. She thanked him for the lift and wished him a pleasant weekend and was surprised when he said casually: 'I'll be here about seven o'clock on Sunday evening—does that suit you?'

'Me?' echoed Polly stupidly. 'Oh, are you going to drive me back too?'

'Unless you had other plans?' He was looking down at her and smiling.

'No, no, I hadn't—I thought Father . . .'

'No need for him to go all that way if I can give you a lift.'

'Well, thank you very much—yes, I'll be ready.'

'I wonder when he's getting married,' mused Mrs Talbot as they watched the Bentley soar up the hill.

'I don't know. I wonder why he's gone that way—I thought he was going to Wells Court.'

'Probably he's taking his fiancée—what's her name? Deirdre—out for the evening. Those sort of people don't start their evenings until late, you know.' She led the way into the house. 'Dinner and dancing,' she went on, 'somewhere posh—black ties and his Deirdre ablaze with diamonds.'

'She doesn't need diamonds,' said Polly soberly. 'She's pretty enough without.'

It would have cheered her up enormously if she could have been with the Professor when he reached his home. Diana was curled up in a chair, reading, taking no notice at all of Deirdre, got up as fine as fivepence and pacing the drawing room floor in a splendid temper.

As he walked in she turned on him. 'Where have you been?' she demanded. 'I've been waiting hours—heaven knows what the Carews will think when we turn up halfway through the soup, and Sir Edward Tomes will be there—he'd be so useful to you, he knows everyone, you'd never want for private patients—and what's he going to think of us?'

The Professor stood by the door, making no attempt to go to her, although he had lifted a hand in greeting to his sister. 'Sir Edward Tomes may think what he likes, and I imagine I can manage my own career without his help. As for the Carews, I've yet to eat a decent dinner there; missing the soup won't worry me.'

'I suppose you were so wrapped up in what you

were doing you forgot about this evening,' Deirdre said waspishly.

He didn't smile, but there was a gleam of laughter in his eyes. 'Something like that,' he agreed lazily. 'Give me fifteen minutes.' He paused at the door. 'You're coming, Diana?'

'Wild horses wouldn't drag me there,' declared his sister, and went back to her book.

Polly, in the bosom of her family, ate Mrs Talbot's excellent supper and regaled them with the week's happenings. 'It's really rather fun,' she ended. 'Hard work, too, but the girls I'm with are very friendly and there's a jolly decent girl on the ward called Freda Honeybun, she's in her second year, but she helps me a lot. Sister's nice too.'

Mrs Talbot dismissed Sister with a wave of the hand. 'And Sam came on to the ward and took you by surprise? I think that's very . . .' she paused and changed what she was going to say, 'interesting. Is he nice with the children?'

'Oh, yes!' Polly's face glowed with the pleasure of talking about him. 'He plays with them and tosses them in the air if they're well enough, and sits on the cots, though it's forbidden.' She saw suddenly that they were all looking at her and ended lamely: 'He doesn't take any notice of me on the ward, only Good morning, Nurse, if he sees me. He really only talks to Sister and Staff Nurse. There's rather a nice houseman called Joseph Taylor.' She trailed the red herring hopefully and her family obligingly swallowed it.

The two days were gone in a flash. Polly filled them from morning until night, taking Shylock for his walk, going down to the village to fetch the groceries for her mother, going to church and stopping afterwards for the usual Sunday gossip in the porch, listening to her two sisters discussing their various boy-friends. They weren't seriously in love with any of them and they joked a lot about them. Polly, listening to them, knew she would never be able to joke about the Professor—more than that, she would never be able to tell anyone about him either; loving him would have to be a life-long secret. Such a pity, she brooded silently, that he has to fall in love with someone who'll never take care of him or look after him when he's tired or comes home late. And I would have: even when he was an irritable old man I would have loved him and made him happy. Only he would have had to love me too, of course, and he doesn't really like me, at least I think not. I daresay he does his duty and offers people lifts and things without really wanting to.

'You've not even been listening,' said Cora suddenly. 'Are you coming home again next week?'

'I expect so, I've got days off on Wednesday and Thursday.'

'Will Sam bring you?'

Polly shook her head. 'Of course not, it was only because he happened to be coming this way that he offered me a lift.'

He was there on the dot of seven o'clock on Sunday evening, but this time he didn't stay even for five minutes, only got out of the car to say a word or two to everyone, but he put Polly's bag in the car and ushered her in too.

She made her goodbyes hurriedly and was annoyed when Cora called: 'See you on Tuesday evening, Polly.'

'It hardly seems worthwhile going back for two days,' observed the Professor. 'Probably you'll have to wait for ten days for the next days off. You enjoyed your weekend?'

'Oh, yes, it was heaven. Did you have a nice time too?'

'No.' He sounded so uncompromisingly brusque that she judged it a good idea to change the conversation. She dwelt on the splendid weather at some length, touched briefly on the garden and asked about the book.

'It'll be published in the autumn,' he told her. 'I must see that you get a copy.' He lapsed into silence and Polly, quite happy just to be sitting beside him, kept quiet, watching the scenery, but presently she said composedly: 'Is this another way to Birmingham? I notice we've left the motorway.'

'I thought we'd have dinner. Would you mind? I missed tea and lunch was so social that there was more talk than food, and I'm famished.'

'Oh, you poor man,' said Polly in a motherly voice. 'Let's find somewhere quickly, it's awful to be hungry.'

His mouth lifted in a smile. 'I hope you're hungry too. There's a quite good place at Cleeve Hill, quite small, just outside Cheltenham and not far out of our way. At what time tonight do you have to be in?'

'Midnight each night.' She went on chattily: 'Of course, you can get a pass for later, only there has to be a good reason.' She stopped abruptly because it might sound to him that she was angling for a date. Nothing had been further from her thoughts and it was palpably absurd in any case, but he was quite likely to turn on her and say something caustic.

He didn't say anything, although he shot a quick glance at her worried profile and smiled.

'They keep a tight rein on you, don't they?' he observed easily. 'But of course, you do have to work hard all day.'

Polly heaved a sigh of relief. They were back on safe ground, and while she was still searching for something to talk about, they arrived at the hotel.

The dining room was elegant, with candlelit tables and shining glass and silver, and the meal was delicious. Polly, her small nose twitching at the delicate fragrance of good food, accepted a glass of sherry and studied the menu, pausing only to say: 'I'm sorry I'm not dressed more suitably, only I didn't know . . .'

Her companion's glance flickered over her pink-clad person. 'You look all right to me,' he observed, giving her the strong impression that he hadn't given her a look until that moment. 'Would you like soup or some sort of starter?'

She decided on avocado pear, stuffed with prawns and bathed in a delicate sauce, and then went on to sole véronique and asparagus, followed by soufflé Harlequin; half chocolate, half vanilla and served with a rich chocolate sauce. Polly ate everything with a splendid appetite and an unselfconscious enjoyment which brought a gleam to the Professor's eyes.

She had no quarrel with the conversation either. For once they were on excellent terms, discussing Greek mythology, the unpredictable behaviour of very small children and the best way to prune roses. She was surprised when she glanced at the clock and saw that it was almost ten o'clock.

The Professor noticed her look. 'Plenty of time,' he said easily, and made no attempt to hurry away. They were almost at the hospital when Polly said: 'Do you live here as well?' And when he didn't answer at once: 'You've never come all this way just to bring me back?'

'I enjoy driving,' he told her blandly. 'Besides, I had to eat somewhere, didn't I?'

'But you could have gone home . . .'

'I spent the weekend there.' His voice dared her to ask any more questions.

He stopped the car outside the hospital entrance and got out with her, carrying her bag and going with her into the vestibule. Someone came in behind them and he said a civil goodnight to Staff Nurse Stockley, who smiled at him and ignored Polly.

'Aren't you two on speaking terms?' he asked Polly.

'Of course, but she's a staff nurse.' She smiled up at him, feeling unexpectedly shy. 'Thank you very much for bringing me back and for the lovely dinner. You'll drive back carefully, won't you?'

His eyes opened wide at that, but he kept the laughter out of his voice. 'I'll remember to do that.' Ignoring the interested face of the night porter in his little office, he bent his head and kissed her lightly.

'We've come a long way, but not quite far enough,' he told her. 'Goodnight, Polly,' and left her gaping after him, not at all sure what he was talking about.

It was fun to find the other girls waiting when she got up to her room. They shared a pot of tea and a rather sleepy gossip, before getting to their beds. They took it for granted that she had been driven back by her father and she didn't correct them; there was no need for anyone to know that she had been in the company of one of the hospital consultants.

But of course, someone did know; she had forgotten Staff. She was making the little beds with her the next morning, trying to keep up with the speedy skill and failing lamentably, when her companion said softly: 'So you cadged a lift, did you?'

Polly, mitreing a corner with care and wholly taken up with getting it right, asked: 'A lift? Where to, Staff?'

'Don't try any of your cheek on me, Nurse Talbot! Coming into the hospital as bold as brass with a consultant! Don't you know that you don't even speak to them?'

Polly said mildly: 'I wasn't on duty.'

'That's got nothing to do with it. Is that why you're going to train here? To get yourself a husband? You won't be the first one, but you listen to me: You'll be the laughing stock of the hospital once this gets around. You'd better watch your step. Spent the evening with him, did you?'

Polly tucked the coverlet in exactly so. 'He happened to be going very near my home and gave me a lift.' Not quite true, she realised, and went red. 'Is that a crime?'

Staff didn't answer that; she said nastily: 'I daresay he's laughing his head off with the other consultants; he knows what hospital gossip is like—not that it bothers him, he's above all that. But you aren't.' She shot Polly a fulminating glance. 'Now go and feed Baby Price and be sure he gets up his wind.'

It was early afternoon before Nurse Honeybun had a chance to speak to Polly. 'What's all this Staff's letting drop, about you and Professor Gervis? Says you went out with him and came in at midnight. I know no one much listens to her, she's such a spiteful cat, anyway, but did you?'

'Well, we came in the door together and she came in just after us, but it wasn't like that at all—I mean, he was only giving me a lift back from home because he was going that way.'

Nurse Honeybun nodded briskly: 'Well, I guessed it was something like that. It's sour grapes; she's been waving her eyelashes at him for ages.'

'But he's going to be married . . .'

Nurse Honeybun's nice horsey face split into a grin. 'You don't really think that would worry her, do you? He's quite a prize, you know.'

It was apparent by supper time that Staff Nurse Stockley had spread her rumours far and wide. Polly, accosted by nurses she had never spoken to before, fended off their questions with good humour and outward patience while she seethed inwardly, aware that no one really believed all Staff's gossip, but it made life more interesting to enjoy scandal, however mild it was.

Polly was quite unprepared for the Professor's round the next morning. He hadn't had one on the previous Tuesday, and she scurried happily round the ward doing her various chores, to slither to a halt as the ward doors opened and he and his party walked in. He and Sister Barnes, his registrar, Staff, Joseph the houseman, the lady social worker, someone from the X-ray department; it looked a crowd. Polly skipped to one side, intent on escaping into the sluice room, but the Professor's voice, loud and clear, stopped her.

'Good morning, Polly. I see you're busy; Sister tells me you're doing quite well.' He smiled down at her. 'I hope you had sufficient sleep on Sunday night? I was rather late bringing you back. By the way, I was on the phone to your father; I told him I'd drive you down tomorrow evening—there's no point in him coming for you when I'm going past your door. Half past six if you can manage it?'

He had spoken casually, making no attempt to lower his voice; everyone was meant to hear. He didn't wait for her to answer, but went on: 'Now, Sister, about Patsy. I'd better have her back in theatre this afternoon—we'll take a look, shall we?'

Polly, safely in the milk kitchen making up feeds with Nurse Honeybun, allowed her thoughts to dwell on the Professor's remarks—meant for all and sundry to hear and establishing without doubt the respectable relationship of old friend's daughter and himself acting as a kindly mentor. It seemed so unlike him that she giggled, and Nurse Honeybun asked what the joke was. 'Nothing,' said Polly. 'I say, how old is Professor Gervis?'

Her companion turned to look at her. 'Don't you know? I mean, if he's a family friend?' She spoke without guile and added: 'He's thirty-six.'

A whole sixteen years older. Her heart gave a sickening lurch at the thought of it. It really was hopeless; she knew she would make him a splendid wife because she loved him with her whole heart, but the odds were against her: Deirdre with her lovely face and gorgeous clothes, her own lack of looks, and now he had let her see quite clearly that he thought of her as someone too young to interest him. Not, she mused, that he would have noticed her if she'd been ten years older.

She filled the last bottle carefully, waited while Nurse Honeybun checked it and went to wash her hands. 'I'll show you how to do the nasal feed,' said her companion. 'Sister says you can have a go at it; she says you're a sensible girl.'

A compliment which should have cheered Polly up, but it didn't.

It was a scramble to be ready by half past six. She had quickly discovered that the off duty written in the book on Sister Barnes' desk and the off duty you actually had were two quite different things. If you were feeding a baby or cleaning a cot and making it up for any little patient who might come in, you finished what you were doing. Polly, helping Staff while she re-dressed a two-year-old's scalded leg, took one quick peep at the clock and saw that it was already long after five-thirty. And Staff wasn't going to let her go and nothing, not even the awful thought that the Professor might get tired of waiting and go without her, would make her ask. She held the toddler quiet in her arms, talking soothingly, while her mind raced ahead. If she got away by six o'clock, she would just be able to do it, and if she was too late, she could phone her father. Perhaps she had better go to the home via the front hall and leave a message with the porter in case the Professor was impatient to leave on time.

Staff finished at last and told her to carry the soiled dressings to the sluice. Polly could see she was going to pretend she had forgotten that Polly was off duty at five o'clock, and it was now ten minutes to six. Unless she could get away within the next few minutes she would have had it.

She hurried down the ward again because Staff was calling for her.

'You'll have to rinse these things through before you put them in the laundry bag—you can go when you've done that, and not before, Nurse Talbot.'

'You may go now, Nurse. Remind me to send you off duty an hour earlier one day. Enjoy your time off.' Sister Barnes' voice was quiet, but there was no gainsaying its authority. Polly escaped in a flurry of thanks.

She showered and changed and flung a few things into her bag, did her face with a speed which would have horrified her sisters, brushed her hair smooth and raced down to the entrance. The Bentley was there, the Professor at the wheel, looking impatient, as well he might; she was five minutes late.

'So sorry,' she began, 'I couldn't get away—you know how it is. I thought you might have gone . . .'

He leaned over and opened the door for her and she got in, breathless with haste and delight at seeing him again. He turned to look at her. 'Sister Barnes off duty?' he asked.

'Yes—at least, when she came on she sent me off, otherwise . . .'

'Staff Nurse Stockley would have kept you for ever.'

'Well, no, I don't suppose so, but she doesn't like me. After all, you can't like everyone, can you?'

'Definitely not. I hope the—er—rumours concerning our relationship have died down?' He watched her redden. 'Staff Nurse Stockley started them off, I believe . . .'

'Well, yes. It was kind of you to make that speech in the ward yesterday: I mean, that you're a friend of Father's and keeping an avuncular eye on me.'

He had started the car and they were in the stream of evening traffic.

His mouth twitched into a smile. 'Ah, yes—the difference in our ages makes everything respectable, doesn't it?'

'I feel a lot older than twenty,' observed Polly 'and I expect you often feel much younger than you really are.'

'Not as often as I should wish.' He found an opening in the traffic and sent the car ahead with effortless speed. 'You're returning on Thursday evening? I'll collect you: I've a lecture to give at the University.'

'Oh, there's no need—it's very kind of you, Professor, but I think—that is, I'm not sure if I ought to . . .'

'Staff Nurse Stockley been needling you? Ignore it, Polly. I do what I like regardless of what people think, and I fancy you're a young woman of spirit. Besides, I can think of nothing sillier than travelling in an empty car and allowing your father to drive to and fro, or worse, you hanging around for buses or trains.' He sounded suddenly rather severe. 'We won't discuss it again.'

This time he didn't stop at her home, merely wished everyone a cheerful good evening and drove off, asking her to be ready by seven o'clock on Thursday.

'It's really very kind of Sam,' murmured Mrs Talbot, watching Polly wolfing her supper. 'Don't they feed you at that hospital, darling? You're a bit pale, or do I mean thinner in the face, or even unhappy?'

'Just hungry,' Polly spoke lightly; she had always scoffed at girls growing thin because they were in love, but it seemed to be true, although she

put in a good deal of exercise each day, going at a
brisk pace up and down the ward from cot to bed
and back again.

It rained the next morning; much needed for
the garden, but such a pity when she had
planned to lie in the garden between a little
weeding and walking Shylock. He had to be
taken for a walk anyway, so she got into an old
mac and took him over the fields regardless of
the weather. The sun shone again the next day,
and since Cora and Marian were free in the
morning, they picked strawberries and peas and
had a picnic lunch on the grass before taking it
in turns to get it cut.

It was just before tea that Diana telephoned to
ask Polly if she would spend her next days off with
her. 'I've got such a lot to talk about and there's
no one—I mean, Sam's a darling, but he doesn't
want to discuss clothes, and Deirdre couldn't care
less. Bob's coming home next week and I do so
want to show someone the things I've bought, so do
come. When are you free?'

'Wednesday and Thursday, and I'd love to come.
Actually I'm free on Tuesday evening.'

'Super—I'm coming to Birmingham one day
next week to have my hair done. I'll make it
Tuesday and we can drive back together.'

'I'm not off until five o'clock, sometimes later,'
Polly told her.

'That suits me fine. I'll be outside about six
o'clock. Be seeing you—'bye till then!'

The Professor wouldn't stop when he called for
her. They were away in five minutes and driving
faster than usual. Polly sensed his preoccupation
and beyond a quiet greeting, stayed silent. She
wasn't sure if he was angry, worried, preoccupied

or what, and it seemed best not to ask. Her patience was rewarded after fifteen minutes or so, for he began to talk in a perfectly normal way about a variety of things, and the subject of Diana's marriage filled the time nicely until he drew up at the hospital.

'Diana's looking forward to seeing you next week.' He was sitting behind the wheel making no attempt to move. 'She'll pick you up, I gather. You will be able to have a good gossip together.'

'Yes, I'm looking forward to it.' She longed to ask him if he'd be there too, but it didn't seem likely. She wanted to ask about his own wedding too; Midsummer Day wasn't far off now; perhaps it was to be a quiet affair, although she thought that unlikely. Deirdre would want her white satin. She sighed unknowingly and he glanced at her downbent head.

'One day you and I will have to have a talk,' he said quietly, and got out of the car and came and opened her door.

What about? wondered Polly. Her work on the ward?—perhaps she wasn't doing as well as she had hoped; certainly Staff complained about her—too slow or too quick or clumsy. The book? That was really all they had in common, and a lot of good a knowledge of Latin and Greek had been, hardly something to attract a man like the Professor to a girl with only passable looks.

She walked beside him to the door and he opened it and stood leaning against it, looking down at her. Suddenly he said: 'Such a pity you have to screw your hair up under that cap.'

Polly was so surprised that she said the first thing that came into her head. 'Well, I have to—I mean, nurses wear caps . . .'

He put out a finger and touched her cheek gently. 'You'll never be a nurse, Polly.' He put her bag into her unresisting hand. 'Goodnight.'

He didn't wait for her reply, which was just as well, because she was speechless.

CHAPTER SIX

POLLY didn't see Professor Gervis for the whole week; at least, he did his rounds and came twice to see a very ill child, but he merely gave her a civil greeting, and as he did the same to all the other nurses on the ward, she could hardly count it as a personal gesture.

A reaction had set in too after the initial excitement of starting her training, the daily routine of feeding, changing nappies, clearing up after the more senior nurses had done dressings, and treatments, and trotting up and down the ward on errands had begun to pall. She had sense enough to know that it was only a passing phase because she was tired and unhappy and that once she had got through the first month or so and had more actual nursing to do she would find her work enjoyable. But always at the back of her mind was the nagging doubt put there by the Professor; that she would never be a nurse. All the more reason to succeed, she told herself, just let him see . . . But he wouldn't be interested; by then he would be a married man with a great many other things to think about.

It didn't do to want something you could never have. She did her best to lose the Professor in busy days and evenings off duty filled by the cinema, fish and chip suppers and long talks over pots of tea in the company of the rest of her set. They had all settled down, but it was nice to have a good grumble among themselves while they copied each other's notes of Sister Tutor's lectures and looked things up in their dictionaries.

'You're lucky,' declared Sally Sims, who was on Children's Medical. 'You've got that glamorous Professor Gervis—you should see Doctor Frost, all of sixty and like a bear with a sore head! He never smiles, not like your Professor. He passed me in the corridor yesterday and said "Good morning, Nurse," just as though he knew me.' She passed her mug for more tea. 'Is he taking you home again this week?'

'No, I'm spending my days off with his sister.'

'Where does she live?' someone asked.

'Well, with Professor Gervis, but she's getting married very soon and I don't know where she's going then.'

'He's going to get married too, isn't he? Perhaps they'll decide to have a double wedding.'

Polly said that she thought not. She couldn't imagine Deirdre sharing her wedding day with anyone, certainly not a girl as pretty as Diana.

She was ready with time to spare on Tuesday evening, but she stayed in her room, fearful that if she went down into the entrance hall, she might see the Professor. As it was, she judged the time nicely and went through the doors just as Diana drew up by them in her Mini.

'This is fun,' said Diana as they shot away from the hospital. 'I've missed you, Polly. If I weren't going to get married very soon I'd make Sam do something about it!'

Polly judged it sensible not to enquire as to what he might do but asked: 'Is your fiancé back yet? You did say this week . . .'

'On Saturday. I'm going up to Heathrow to meet his plane—he'll stay with us, of course, until

we've got all our plans settled. He's got a flat in
London and a dear little house on the Thames
about ten miles this side of Maidenhead, so we
shan't have to house-hunt. And I bought my
wedding dress today; I hadn't intended to, I'd
planned to go to London, but there's a boutique
that's quite good and I went along to have a look
for another cotton dress, and there it was—just
what I wanted! You shall see it when we get home.
I bought a few more things too—I'll try them on
after dinner. Sam won't be there, so we can do
what we like.'

Polly swallowed disappointment. Of course he
wouldn't be there; he wouldn't be there as he
would be with Deirdre, making his own plans. She
said casually: 'I expect he's busy too. Is he getting
married after you or before?'

Diana clashed her gears and made great work of
overtaking another car before she answered. 'I
should think it would be soon, knowing him.'

'And Deirdre wants to be married on
Midsummer Day, and that's next week, isn't it?'

'Not a hope of that,' said Diana flatly. 'Now tell
me what you think of hospital life.'

So Polly described her day, leaving out the dull
parts and making Diana laugh a good deal over
the mistakes she had made. 'I don't think I'm
going to be much good,' she said finally.

'Don't tell me you hanker after your Greek and
Latin?'

'Oh, no—the children and babies are great, and
when I've been there longer I'll get very interesting
jobs to do, not just feeds and moppings up and
taking things to the Path Lab.'

Jeff came to the door as they got out of the car
and greeted her with dignified pleasure. 'A

pleasure to see you again, miss, and Bessy says the
same. I'll take in the parcels, Miss Diana, and put
the car away. Bessy wants to know if you'd like
dinner a little earlier than usual.'

'Yes, please, Jeff. I'm famished and I'm sure
Miss Talbot is too. We'll tidy ourselves and come
straight down—ten minutes or so?'

Polly had the room she had been given
previously and someone had put a bowl of early
roses on the table by the window. She sniffed at
them and stood looking out at the garden below.
It was a riot of colour now in the evening sun.
Tomorrow morning, before breakfast, she would
go down to the little stream; perhaps the dogs
would like to go with her.

The evening passed pleasantly, with Diana
prancing around in the clothes she had bought,
ending with the wedding dress; seeing her floating
round the bedroom in yards of white organza and
lace, Polly felt a pang of envy. She smothered it at
once; envy got you nowhere, only made you
unhappy and discontented. She offered genuine
admiration, helped Diana to pack everything away
in layers of tissue paper and went downstairs again
for more coffee before bedtime.

She was up early the next morning, wandering
round the garden with the dogs, and after
breakfast she and Diana played tennis until they
were tired, then swam lazily in the pool before
lunch, and since it was unusually hot for early
June, they lay on the velvet turf behind the house
until Jeff brought tea to them. It was just before
dinner that Diana was called to the phone; she was
gone for several minutes and returned looking
pleased with herself. Polly supposed it had been
some kind of news about Bob, but presently Diana

mentioned that he would be unable to send her a message of any sort until Friday, which left Polly in a fever of curiosity; it might have been from Sam. For the hundredth time she wondered where he was and almost choked herself in her efforts not to ask.

And Diana didn't mention him once for the whole of that evening, and although she had a great deal to say about everything under the sun while they lounged in the garden the next day, she had nothing to say about her brother. It turned sultry and dark after lunch and thick clouds began rolling across the horizon. Polly watched them creeping nearer, sure there would be a storm. As they had their tea she said: 'Look, Diana, how about us leaving earlier than you intended? I hate to go, but the weather's looking awful and if we went now, you'd be back before the storm breaks—or at least I hope so.'

But Diana wouldn't hear of it. 'What's a few thunderclaps?' she wanted to know carelessly. 'You've still got to look at that outfit I bought— the one I'm not sure I like. We'll do that before dinner and I'll drive you back directly afterwards.'

Thunder was growling in the distance as they got into the Mini, and just as Diana switched on Jeff came hurrying out. 'That's Mr Sam on the telephone, Miss Diana, he says you're not to drive Miss Talbot back, but to wait here and he'll take her later on. He doesn't like the look of the weather.'

Polly, who didn't like the look of it either, heaved a sigh of relief which turned into a soundless groan at Diana's airy: 'Tell him I've already left, Jeff, say Polly wanted to leave early, insisted on leaving.'

She waved to the frustrated Jeff and raced down the drive. 'Well, you did want to leave early, didn't you, Polly?' She gave a giggle. 'And why should he be so fussy suddenly?'

Polly didn't reply. She had a nasty feeling that something dire was going to happen, but it wouldn't be any good arguing with Diana, that young lady, while not bearing any physical resemblance to her brother, had more than her share of his high-handed manner and like him, took it for granted that she should have her own way. All the same, she suggested mildly: 'Won't there be less traffic if we go through Evesham and Redditch?'

'I feel like a bit of fast driving, we'll go up the M5. I'll be there and back home before Sam gets back.'

'Is he at the hospital?' asked Polly carelessly.

'He's got a date with Deirdre, he won't be home for hours.' Diana drove some miles in silence while the sky grew darker and darker, split by occasional flashes of lightning. Presently she said: 'Good, here's the motorway, now I can put my foot down.'

Which she did, undeterred by the sudden torrent of rain which blotted out everything ahead of them. It was dark by now and the lights from other cars danced to and fro, distorted in the rainswept windscreen. Diana was going too fast but Polly kept silent. Polly sensed she was not in a mood to be thwarted. She hoped she would slow down when she discovered that Polly was apparently undisturbed. She was doing a steady seventy now and, Polly had to admit, driving superbly. All the same, she was being overtaken and was forced to slow as two cars, far too close, shot past her. They were a hundred yards ahead, barely discernible in the driving rain, when the second car rammed the one ahead. Even above the roar of the rain they heard the screech of torn metal and a moment later saw a sheet of flame.

'Get on to the shoulder and pull up, Diana!' Polly spoke urgently, her head over her shoulder watching to see how close the following cars were. They should be able to manage it, only they wouldn't be able to slow down too much or there would be a pile-up. She gave a quick glance ahead; the flames had enveloped both cars and other cars were already tangled, some stopping, some trying to get past.

'I feel sick,' said Diana. 'I'll have to stop.'

Polly didn't waste time talking about it; she leaned across Diana, got her hands on the wheel and her feet clumsily on to the pedals, slowed just a little and got on to the hard shoulder. She wasn't the only one there, but it seemed the safest place for the moment. Diana was lying back, very white, her eyes closed. 'Oh, God, I feel ghastly!' she whispered. 'Those cars . . .'

Polly felt sick herself, but it wouldn't do for both of them to pass out. 'Yes, I know—it's ghastly they couldn't have known anything about it, though. The thing is, there's a right old mess ahead of us; we're going to be here for a long time. Do you feel a little better?'

'No.' Diana sounded tearful, but she managed to say: 'I didn't know you could drive a car.'

'Well, I'm no good at it, but one of Cora's boy-friends showed me how and let me drive once or twice.'

Diana sniffed: 'What are we going to do, Polly?'

'Wait here. The police will come and sort us out,

but they've other things to see to first.' She flinched at the vivid lightning and thunderclap above their heads; thunderstorms made her feel nervous, and the frightful accident she had just seen had reduced her nerves to twanging point. Normally she was a calm, unflappable girl, but when there was a sharp rap on her window she was to be forgiven for giving an instantly suppressed shriek.

She wound down the window with a shaking hand and the Professor stuck his head inside. There was another flash of lightning as he did so, and all Polly could see of him was a face as dark as the sky above them, his hair plastered to his head, his mouth set grimly.

He said in a soft furious voice: 'You see what trouble you've caused by your stubborn insistence on leaving? I thought better of you. Is Diana hurt?' He added even more softly: 'I should like to wring your neck!'

Polly turned to look at her. Diana had, unbelievably, gone to sleep. She said: 'No, she's not hurt.' She was still registering his words with a disbelief which didn't allow her to answer him. She said in a voice as quiet as his own: 'Is your car here?'

'Yes, a few hundred yards behind this one. As soon as I had Diana's message I followed you.'

She uttered her thoughts out loud. 'You were with Deirdre.'

'Yes. Stay there, I'm going to carry Diana back to the Bentley. Thank God she had the sense to drive on to the hard shoulder. I'll come back for you presently.'

'There's no need.' Polly kept her voice steady, fighting a desire to give way to screaming hysterics. 'I'll go along to a police car and get a lift in to the hospital—there'll be plenty of ambulances.'

He gave a harsh laugh. 'Don't be a little fool—you've been the cause of enough trouble as it is. You'll do as I say.'

Polly remained silent while he went round the car, opened Diana's door and lifted her out. She opened her eyes briefly, said: 'Hullo there,' and closed them again. Polly envied her; it would be marvellous to go to sleep and wake up to find that she had been having a nightmare.

She closed the door after the Professor and his burden, picked up her overnight bag, locked the other door and got out; she didn't dare lock that door too in case Diana hadn't got the key on her. Through the rain she could see the Professor's broad back already some distance away, but she didn't wait, but began to make her way along the side of the motorway until she was level with the smouldering heap of metal, surrounded by a haphazard medley of cars. There was no traffic, of course, so she crossed to the centre of the motorway and went straight to a police car parked there. They were kind and helpful, and although she had to wait while they took her name and where she worked and asked a few questions as to what she had seen, presently she was ushered into the front seat of one of the ambulances. The first to leave, she discovered thankfully, taking two seriously injured men to hospital. She was no sooner perched between the two ambulance men than they were away.

'Nasty smash up, miss,' commented the driver. 'You're a nurse, are you?'

'Yes, a student nurse at the children's hospital. We were a few hundred yards behind the cars

when they crashed.' Just for a moment Polly felt
sick, remembering. 'It was awful . . . I suppose the
people in the cars . . .?'

'No chance at all. Quite a few hurt, though;
couldn't stop in time, you see, or braked and
had the car behind run into them. In this
weather too.'

The other man asked: 'On your own, were you,
love?'

'No, a friend was driving me, but she's gone
back to her home with her brother, there wasn't
any point in her waiting to take me the rest of the
way. They'll take hours to get the traffic going
again, won't they?'

'You're right there. Will you be all right if we
take you to the General? Can you find your way to
the children's hospital on your own?'

'Oh yes. I'll be glad of the walk, it'll make
everything more normal.' Polly smiled with a
shaking mouth. 'I keep thinking of those poor
people in the cars.'

'They wouldn't have known, ducks. You get on
back and have a good hot cuppa and then go to
bed, you'll feel better about it in the morning.'

They had reached the hospital and she wished
them a hasty goodbye and thanked them before
slipping away. The main streets were close by, so
she caught a bus which would take her most of the
way and sat, wedged between a thin, ladylike
woman and a fat man reading his paper. There
was an elderly man with a cross face sitting
opposite her; they all three glanced at her and then
hastily away, looking irritated. None of them
approved of a young woman who cried in public,
especially when she made no attempt to stop, just
let the tears run down her cheeks. They exchanged

indignant glances when she got off the bus and watched her hurry off into the rain.

She had stopped crying by the time she reached the hospital doors. The porter looked up as she crossed the hall and then came out of his office to speak to her. 'Nurse Talbot, Professor Gervis phoned—three times—wanting to know if you were here.' He looked at her blotchy face worriedly. 'He said there's been an accident. You're not hurt? Shall I get Home Sister?'

'No, Griggs, it's quite all right, thanks. There was an accident on the motorway, just ahead of us, but we got off the road in time. Two cars— they caught fire.' Polly caught her breath. 'Quite a few people were hurt because the other cars couldn't stop or braked too hard. Luckily Professor Gervis was in his car behind us—I was with his sister—her brother took her home and I got a lift in an ambulance. If he should ring again would you tell him I'm back and perfectly all right?' She managed a smile. 'Goodnight, Griggs.'

He went back to his office and rang over to the Nurses' Home and asked for Home Sister, so that by the time Polly got there, that lady was waiting for her. 'Tea,' she said briskly, 'a warm bath and bed, and you'll have a sleeping pill whether you want it or not.'

So Polly sat in Sister's comfortable room and drank cup after cup of tea, then she went over the whole disaster again and presently went to her room, where she was gently fussed over until she was in bed, the pill swallowed, and instructed not to get up in the morning if she felt the least bit poorly.

But a night's sleep put her back on her sensible feet once more. She went down to breakfast, a little pale and quiet but glad to work. It was Nurse Honeybun who told her during the morning that Professor Gervis had rung Sister Bates to ask if Polly was on duty and none the worse for her experience. And later, while she was feeding one of the babies, Sister had come and sat down beside her and asked her if she felt all right. 'Because that was a nasty thing to happen, Nurse, and it takes time to get over the shock, but perhaps you'd rather work?'

'Yes, Sister, I would, and I'm quite all right.'

'Good. Your lecture has been changed this afternoon, it will be at four o'clock instead of the usual time, so come back on to the ward after your dinner and go off duty straight from the lecture room.'

There was a good deal of talk about the accident during dinner. Polly, sitting with her own set, was deeply grateful to them for not having much to say about it—indeed, they talked, rather selfconsciously, about everything but that, although she was well aware that they were dying to hear about it. She went back to the ward with the kindly Nurse Honeybun and started on the dull job of putting away the clean laundry from the baskets stacked on the landing. At first she had Nurse Honeybun with her, but presently she was called away and Polly went on stacking sheets and towels, endless nappies, baby garments and a miscellany of toddler's clothes. She was in the linen cupboard, counting bibs, when the door, standing ajar, was pushed open and the Professor came in.

At the sight of him her heart stopped and then began to dance around beneath her ribs. There was nothing in the blandness of his handsome face to suggest that he was angry, but his eyes were dark and cold. Dear, tiresome, bad-tempered man, she thought lovingly, and at the same time, the sharp memory of the stark anger on his face when he had found them in the car, and the nasty things he had said to her, sparked off her own usually mild temper. If he had come to apologise, she was going to make it difficult for him.

She couldn't have been more mistaken. He closed the door behind him and stood looking at her, so that she felt impelled to say something.

She had herself nicely in hand by now; her voice was its usual pleasant self, if a bit wooden. 'You want to see Sister, sir? I'll fetch her.'

But that was no use; he ignored that. He said in a voice as cold as his eyes: 'What possessed you to go deliberately against my wishes and persuade Diana to bring you back? The ever-present instinct to annoy me?'

She sat down on a convenient pile of pillows, her hands tidily in her lap, and stared back at him. So Diana hadn't told him that it was she who had disregarded his message, in which case there wasn't anything to be done.

'Is Diana all right?' she asked, and watched him contain impatient anger.

'She was put to bed and given a sedative, she was sleeping when I went to see her this morning.' He smiled nastily. 'Trailing red herrings, Polly? It won't do, you know.' He gave her a long intent look. 'You could have been killed, the pair of you! Even if you don't drive a car you must know that heavy rain after a dry spell makes the roads treacherous—not only that, you could see for yourself that there was a bad storm breaking, and you prevailed upon Diana to ignore my message!'

Polly said nothing but stared down at her hands,

her mouth tightly shut for fear she should start explaining, and even if she did, he might think that she was making excuses, hiding behind Diana, telling tales.

The Professor fetched a deep sigh. 'I should like to shake you until your bones rattle,' he observed with some heat.

Polly got to her feet. 'I'm afraid you'll have to wait for that,' she told him politely. 'I have to go to a lecture at four o'clock, and it's five minutes to.' She swept her small person past him with what dignity she could muster, seeing that it was a tight squeeze to get to the door. Her hand on the handle, she said with a calm she didn't feel: 'I promise you I'll keep out of your way in future. My only regret is that I've started my training at this hospital; I had thought I would never have to see you again.'

A splendid exit line, marred by his hand on her arm preventing her from leaving.

'You don't mean that, Polly.' His voice was so gentle that she nearly choked on the lie.

'Oh, but I do . . .' She couldn't trust herself to say any more, but pulled away from his hand and scurried to Sister's Office to ask to go to the lecture.

Sister Bates eyed her thoughtfully. Polly Talbot had all the attributes of a good nurse, besides that she wasn't one of the flighty careless girls she had to cope with from time to time, but now she looked wild-eyed, and as white as her apron. She wondered what Professor Gervis had been saying to her. Sister Bates, who had a sentimental regard for him, wished she knew. She watched Polly slip away and close the door after her very quietly. Hardly the Professor's type, perhaps, but surely better than that haughty piece he had brought to the ward at Christmas. Sister Bates, who cherished her little patients fiercely, had found it hard to forgive Deirdre's fastidious rejection of eager small faces and sticky fingers. She shook her head sadly at the Professor's blindness, for he loved the children in his care and she very much doubted if the fashionable creature who had accompanied him would want them.

Polly sat through her lecture, looking attentive, making notes which she was quite unable to decipher afterwards, and when Sister Tutor's eagle eye registered her pale face, assuring that lady that she felt very well.

Indeed she substantiated this statement by going to the cinema with her friends after tea and then held a tea-party in her room afterwards with several pots of tea and bags of chips from the fish and chip shop down the street. She, who had been considered rather quiet, was the life and soul of the party.

But later, in bed, she cried herself to sleep. She had nothing to cry about, she told herself repeatedly; she had known for weeks—since she had first met him—that the Professor didn't like her, so why was she making a fuss now? She knew he was quite entitled to be angry, since he thought that it was her fault that Diana had ignored his message. She shut her eyes and wished for sleep, and instead remembered that Midsummer Day would have been his wedding day if Deirdre had had her way. She slept at length, imagining the horrid girl in yards of white satin and chiffon. As she dozed off she muttered: 'Oh, my poor Sam!'

There was a letter for her the next morning; an expensive, thick envelope containing an invitation

to Diana's wedding and a note with it. 'I'll never
forgive you if you don't come!'

Polly put it in her pocket. Of course she
wouldn't go; she had nothing to wear and she
would feel a fool, knowing no one there. Besides,
hadn't she told the Professor that she would keep
out of his way?

Not so very difficult. She saw him often enough,
crossing the courtyard, driving away in the
Bentley, standing in a corridor talking to a
colleague, and after two more days, on the ward,
doing his round, but he gave no sign that he had
even seen her, and on the ward it was easy enough
to make for the sluice or the feed kitchen and stay
there until he had gone again. In one more day she
would have her days off again and there were no
more rounds for four days, only the Registrar
coming each morning and Joseph who came
several times a day, whenever Sister Bates needed
him. Polly liked him; he wasn't a great deal older
than she was and a little uncertain of himself. On
the round, she had noticed that he hung on the
Professor's every word and copied the way he put
his hands in his pockets while he talked to his
patients, and once, when she was holding a toddler
so that he might examine a small labouring chest,
she had asked if he liked Professor Gervis. Joseph
had broken into a eulogy of praise which lasted for
quite some time. 'He's—well, I can't think of a
word. I've been to his house once or twice, you
know—we had a smashing dinner and he—he
listened when I talked. He's great!'

Sitting with a small baby on her lap while he
peered carefully down a small ear, he told her that
he'd been invited to Diana's wedding. 'I met her
when I went there,' he explained. 'I haven't got a

decent suit, but I suppose I can hire one. I don't know anyone much there, but I'd like to go.'

He added: 'He won't be in today.'

Which in a way was a relief to Polly; she was free to go up and down the ward and through the hospital on various errands without peering around to make sure he wasn't in sight. She told herself how glad she was and longed for him to come through the door.

Which he did an hour later, with Sister Bates in full sail beside him and Staff hovering. There was no escape this time either, for Polly was on her way up the ward with a toddler in floods of tears, and to turn tail and run just wasn't possible.

The Professor appeared not to see her, already bending over a small boy who had been admitted with a badly scalded arm. She put the tearful child into his cot, arranged toys suitably, locked the cot sides and made for the door. The linen cupboard, she thought rapidly, although it had no pleasant memories for her, or the kitchen. She was at the door when Nurse Honeybun stopped her. 'Polly,' she hissed from one of the beds on the other side of the ward, 'get some sheets from the trolley, will you, and look sharp!'

She stayed to help, making up a fresh bed while Nurse Honeybun cradled a drowsy little girl on her lap. They had just tucked her in once more when the Professor's party came back, reinforced by Joseph, still apologising because he hadn't known the Professor was there. They drew level with Polly and she bent over the trolley, tidying the already tidy pile of linen, wishing herself invisible.

To no avail, for the Professor stopped beside her. 'You are coming to Diana's wedding, Polly?' he asked. So very unfair of him, knowing she would have to speak to him with so many people gaping at her.

'I'm afraid not, sir.' She tried to sound calm and polite and succeeded in being frigidly wooden. 'I'm on duty.'

A mistake, she realised the moment the words were out of her mouth, for he said smoothly: 'Oh, I'm sure Sister Bates can remedy that, can you not, Sister? Diana will be disappointed—besides, Joseph has been invited and you could come together. We shall look forward to seeing you both.'

Polly looked at him then, her eyes with their long lashes, dark with temper, and found him smiling, daring her to refuse. She said in a high voice, 'Thank you, sir,' and could have slapped Joseph's pleased face when he said cheerfully: 'I say, sir, that'll be great—I mean going with someone I know.'

The whole party moved on, leaving Polly fuming and Nurse Honeybun frankly envious.

Polly's father drove her home that evening and the family received the news of the wedding with a good deal of interest. 'Laura Ashley,' chorused her sisters. 'We will take you tomorrow—Cheltenham.' They fixed their father with compelling eyes. 'Father, you'll drive us there?'

'Well, I am free . . .'

'Good. Now, Polly . . .'

'I'll go to Laura Ashley, but I want to choose for myself—something quite plain.'

Her sisters made faces. 'Oh, Polly—all right!'

But the next day they had to admit that they could find no fault with her choice; a skirt and jacket in very pale pink, the skirt full and tucked, the jacket short with a little stand-up collar, and since it was a wedding she bought a white spotted lawn blouse with a good deal of fine lace. It took some searching to find the hat she liked, a pale pink straw with a fairly wide brim and a neat ribbon. Low-heeled shoes, pale gloves and a handbag borrowed from Cora completed the outfit and left her pocket almost empty, but as Marian pointed out, she would shortly be getting her first month's salary and what she had bought was worth every penny. She went back to the hospital burdened with her purchases, dreaming impossible dreams about the Professor, his calm shaken at the sight of her, falling in love. And that's nonsense, she told herself crossly, when he's already in love with Deirdre. She dreaded seeing them together at the wedding, but at least she had the time to get used to the idea; she would be serene and pleasantly cool if she had to speak to them, and she didn't see how she could avoid it.

On the day of the wedding Joseph drove her down in his battered Ford, uneasy in his hired suit. He had taken one look at her in her finery and said: 'Good lord, I hardly know you, you look quite pretty!' a left-handed compliment which left her giggling.

But they sobered up as they reached the church. The lanes leading to it were lined with cars, Rolls and Bentleys and Mercedes and Jaguars. Joseph inched his Ford into a space between a Rolls Corniche and a Bristol and got out. 'I say,' he said worriedly, 'this is all a bit above us, isn't it?'

'Pooh,' declared Polly, 'of course it isn't. Weddings are for everyone, and besides, I daresay most of these cars are company cars.' She put on her gloves. 'Let's go, Joseph.'

The usher showed them to seats halfway down the church, already well filled with guests and

most of the village. The tall man standing at the
chancel steps must be Bob, Polly decided. He
looked nice, but at the moment nervous, but
then who wouldn't be? There were some gorgeous
outfits in the pews and a number of older men
with noses just like the Professor. Uncles, and the
self-assured ladies with them would be aunts.
There was a fair sprinkling of young people too,
wearing the sort of clothes to make Polly's own
outfit look exactly what it was—off the peg, even
if pretty.

There was a little stir at the back of the church
and Deirdre, with an elderly couple behind her,
came down the aisle. She was wearing a vivid
yellow outfit and a hat with a large wavy brim and
a load of pink silk roses round its crown. The
colour scheme was arresting but not altogether
pleasing, although it was obvious from Deirdre's
expression that she was very pleased with herself.

'Who's the glamorous beanpole?' whispered
Joseph.

'She's Professor Gervis's fianceé.' It helped quite
a bit when he muttered: 'I don't believe it, you're
having me on.' He stopped because Polly had dug
him in the ribs; the Professor was coming down
the aisle with an old lady dressed richly in an out-
of-date garment and crowned with a feather toque.
Granny? wondered Polly silently. She had the
same nose and the same air of being quite sure of
herself. She craned her neck to see where they were
sitting, but they were too far away in the little
church and a forest of hats obscured her view. The
bridesmaids were in the porch, she could hear silky
rustlings and urgent whisperings, and presently the
organist let himself go in a loud burst of music as
Diana, looking quite lovely, came down the aisle

on the arm of an elderly man. That would be
Uncle George, decided Polly, who had listened for
hours to Diana's plans and had a good memory for
names. The bridesmaids were small, and made a
charming picture, walking carefully, peeping
sideways to see if their mothers were watching.
Pretty, well brought up children, not like the little
sick creatures in Sister Bates' ward.

The service was short; in no time at all the
register was being signed while the congregation
murmured and rustled and coughed and then rose
to its feet as the bride and groom started down the
aisle, and behind them the old lady and Professor
Gervis. Polly, safely anonymous among so many
guests, allowed herself the pleasure of watching
him. Morning dress suited him and he wore it
unselfconsciously, and he was a good head taller
than the other men around him. He bent his head
to listen to his companion, answered her and
looked up, straight at Polly. She didn't look away
because that would have been silly, but she didn't
smile either, only looked at him with her heart in
her eyes. Just for a moment he smiled briefly, and
Joseph said happily: 'I say, Professor Gervis saw
us, didn't he? What do we do next?'

'Wait,' said Polly sensibly, while her heart's beat
slowly returned to normal. 'When all the family
have gone we can go too and drive to the house. I
know the way.'

Joseph caught her arm. 'I say, there's that girl
again—what a bad-tempered piece she is, too. I
hope I don't have to meet her.'

'Very unlikely,' said Polly positively and
erroneously. 'Come along, we can go now.'

CHAPTER SEVEN

POLLY and Joseph were the very last guests to
arrive at the house because the Ford hadn't
wanted to start. Jeff, stationed at the open door,
ushered them into the hall with a welcoming smile
and a 'Nice to see you, Miss Talbot.' He waved
them into the drawing-room where the bride and
groom, the old lady, Professor Gervis and Deirdre
were standing together as the last of the guests
went to join everyone else. Feeling conspicuous,
they crossed the room, to be welcomed by Diana's
pleased: 'There you are, Polly, how pretty you
look.' She kissed Polly's rather flushed cheek and
turned to Joseph. 'And you can kiss me,' she
invited him. 'Polly, this is Bob—Bob, she's the
dearest creature.'

Polly shook hands and murmured conventional
phrases, aware that Sam's eyes were on her. She
had to look at him then, because he touched her
arm lightly and said: 'Grandmother, this is Polly
Talbot, a friend of Diana's and training to be a
children's nurse. She's also something of a
scholar.'

Polly shook hands again very gently, for the old
lady was indeed old, with bony fingers loaded with
rings. But the blue eyes she fixed on Polly were still
bright and sharp. 'Now that's a nice change,' she
observed in a carrying voice. 'Most young women
of today seem to think of nothing but starving
themselves and buying silly clothes.' Her look
raked Polly. 'You're very nicely dressed, gal, and

you've got a shape too.' She switched her gaze to her grandson. 'Isn't that so, Sam?' And before he could answer: 'Of course I shouldn't have asked you that with Deirdre here. I expect you two young women have met?' she asked wickedly.

'Yes, we have,' said Polly pleasantly, and gave Deirdre a thin edge of a smile. 'Weddings are such fun, aren't they? I expect you're looking forward to yours?' Egged on by some mischievous urge, she looked up at the Professor. 'You too, of course, Professor Gervis.'

She was a little put out to see that he was hiding laughter. Dismay caught her by the throat. Perhaps he and Deirdre were already married—Midsummer Day had come and gone; they could have got married very quietly and not told anyone outside the family. Her eyes flew to Deirdre's left hand, lying rather ostentatiously on his sleeve. There was only an engagement ring on her finger. Polly heaved a sigh of relief while the Professor, reading her telltale face, concealed amusement.

Joseph was still talking to old Mrs Gervis and Bob and Diana called across them. 'I've never asked you how you felt after that horrid accident. Sam said you'd got back to the hospital, but didn't you feel ghastly? And it was all my fault, rushing off like that. You know I never did like doing what I was told, Sam . . .' She looked at him and laughed. 'That's why I said Polly made me go back. She didn't, of course. I'd have been lost without her, you know, I felt so sick and giddy, and she got on to the hard shoulder although she can't drive. But she'd have told you all that . . .' She turned to speak to her grandmother, and Joseph, released from the old lady's sharp questions, turned thankfully to the Professor and

Deirdre. Neither of them seemed disposed to say much, and he was glad of Polly's hand on his arm as they moved away to mingle with the other guests.

There was a marquee on the lawn behind the house and people were strolling around the garden while others were at the buffet arranged on three sides of the marquee. 'Let's eat,' begged Joseph. 'I say, I'm glad that's over, that old lady turned me inside out—and what's the matter with Professor Gervis? Hardly spoke to me, and that awful girl with him looked at me as though I'd gatecrashed.'

Polly gave him an encouraging pat. 'Don't worry, Joseph, I daresay Professor Gervis will talk to you presently, and Deirdre is like that with everyone! I'm famished, let's pile our plates and find a quiet corner.'

They knew very few people there; consultants and their wives from the hospital, who nodded affably to Joseph and just looked at Polly, and the Professor's Registrar, who passed the time of day with him, smiled at Polly and said he felt sure they had met before and then gaped in astonishment when she said sweetly: 'Well, yes, we have. On the ward, you know.'

His 'Good God!' she took to be a compliment to her appearance.

The food was delicious—salmon patties, vol-au-vents, tiny sausage rolls, minute sandwiches which Joseph ate three at a time, little pancakes filled with prawns, iced cakes, ice creams, strawberries and cream, jellies and creams, and all the champagne imaginable. 'This must have cost the earth,' declared Joseph, 'but of course, he can afford it. She's a smasher, isn't she? Diana, I mean.'

'Yes, and such a nice person. I'm lucky to have her for a friend. Bob looks nice too.' She looked around her. 'I expect they'll cut the cake presently.'

She accepted more champagne, nibbled at the cake, toasted the happy pair and listened to the speeches. Uncle Tom took a long time over his, the groom was brief, saying all the right things nicely, and the best man was pleasantly witty. Polly, whose shoes were beginning to pinch her, was relieved when Diana slipped away to change, leaving the guests to relax and gossip. Perhaps they could find a quiet corner of the garden for ten minutes and she could sit in her stockinged feet. She was on the point of suggesting this to Joseph when she was frustrated by the Professor appearing apparently from the ground beside them. 'Sorry I haven't had the time to have a chat,' he said to Joseph, 'but I do hope you've enjoyed it so far. Weddings are really a woman's business, aren't they? Once people start to go we might get a chance for a word. In the meantime, I've a young cousin who wants to meet you . . .' He turned his head and a pretty girl in her late teens came towards them. 'Jane, there's Joseph, take him away for ten minutes and pick his brains—she's decided she wants to be a surgeon, see if you can put her off. But don't miss the going away party.'

Polly stood helplessly watching, wishing with all her heart that there was just one person she knew there to whom she could turn. But there wasn't. She began to walk away as nonchalantly as possible, to be caught and held in a firm grip. 'And now, my girl, we can have our little talk,' observed the Professor.

'We have nothing to talk about,' said Polly briskly, 'and there's someone I see over there . . .'

He had brought her to an unwilling halt and was looking down at her bent head. 'No, there isn't—you know as well as I that you don't know anyone here except Deirdre, and I hardly expect you to go out of your way to find her.'

'That's a beastly thing to say!'

'Yes, isn't it? Polly, why didn't you tell me? Why did you let me think it was you? You had only to say . . .'

'The very last thing I would have done,' she told him waspishly. 'You were in such a foul temper that you wouldn't have believed me—besides, I don't tell tales on my friends.'

He said quite humbly: 'If I apologise could we at least say good morning when we meet? I'm more sorry than I can say; it wouldn't do any good at present to tell you why I was so angry, but if you will forgive me I'll promise to count ten before I lose my temper again.'

Something in his voice made her look at him. He was tired and worried and she wondered why, but when he smiled she forgot that. 'Of course I forgive you,' she said bracingly, 'and I must say I'm glad to have it settled, it's so hard to keep out of your way in the hospital.'

He gave a great shout of laughter. 'Oh, my dear girl—I've been forcibly put in mind of the White Rabbit on several occasions; brief glimpses of you rushing off to hide in the sluice or round the next corner!' His eyes searched her face. 'One day soon, we must have a talk.' He wasn't laughing now and because he was looking at her so intently she said hastily: 'Oh, about Sir Ronald's book,' but he didn't answer her at once and when he did all he said was: 'You look so pretty, Polly, prettier than anyone else here.'

She goggled at him, as pink as her dress. 'Oh, but I'm not,' she assured him. 'It's only Laura Ashley, you know, and everyone else is in haute couture.'

'Are they? I wouldn't know, and if that's Laura Ashley, whoever or whatever that is, then she or it deserves a medal.'

Polly beamed up at him. 'It's a her, she makes lovely clothes for women with no money—well, comparatively speaking, that is.'

'He was laughing again. 'Are you flat broke?'

'Very nearly, but it's almost payday.' And that reminded her of something. 'You said I'd never be a nurse,' she remarked. 'You didn't mean it, did you?'

His face wasn't tired or worried any more but blandly friendly. 'Oh, yes, I did. We'll discuss that some time.'

Polly had gone quite pale. 'But I like it, and Sister Bates says I'm doing quite well, and there's nothing else I want to be.'

'That's something else we have to discuss.' He smiled down at her and then raised his head to look over her shoulder. 'Here's Deirdre,' he observed. He didn't sound pleased but he didn't sound annoyed either. 'Are they ready to leave?' he asked as she reached them.

'Yes, just about. I've been looking for you everywhere, Sam. What will people think?'

'About what, Deirdre?' He sounded uninterested, and she said crossly: 'We are engaged, you know.' She shot a look at Polly. 'Where's that boy you were with?'

Polly had no chance to open her mouth before

the Professor said silkily: 'Joseph? That boy is going to be a very good paediatrician one day.'

'And I suppose Polly is going to be an equally good nurse?' sneered Deirdre.

'On the contrary,' he ignored Polly's flabbergasted look, 'there's no chance of that. Ah, here are Jane and Joseph; we'd all better go into the house, I suppose.'

And once there, he was instantly caught up in various groups of family and friends. Polly could see him, head well above everyone else's, moving round the drawing room with Deirdre trying to keep beside him.

Diana and Bob came downstairs then and everyone surged into the hall and out on to the sweep where Bob's car stood. There was a great throwing of confetti and rose-petals and a good deal of laughing and hand-shaking and kissing. Polly, standing on the edge of things with Joseph beside her, was surprised when Diana broke away from a circle of friends and flung her arms around her. 'We'll be back in three weeks and I'll see you then; you must come and stay.' She bent to whisper in Polly's ear: 'Doesn't Deirdre look absolutely frightful? Just like Birds' custard before it's cooked!' She kissed Polly's cheek, blew a kiss at Joseph and flitted away. A moment later she and Bob had roared away, balloons billowing from the back of the car.

Everyone stood around talking for a bit and presently Polly said: 'I think we could go, Joseph, don't you?' And when he looked a bit crestfallen: 'Oh, I expect you want to say goodbye to Jane. I wonder where she is?'

Not far away, in fact, coming towards them with the Professor in her wake. 'Joseph, come into my study; these two can have a chat over a cup of tea for ten minutes.'

And Joseph went willingly, leaving Polly and Jane standing there, but only for a moment, for Jeff, hard on their heels, had found two chairs and was offering cups of tea.

'My feet are killing me,' declared Polly.

'So are mine,' Jane grinned at her. 'I say, he's a dear, isn't he?'

'Joseph?' asked Polly carefully, and was glad she had got it right. 'Yes, he is. He's marvellous with children too, and nice to us—you know, the student nurses. Some of the doctors don't take any notice of us at all, but he's friendly.'

'I'd like to be a surgeon,' said Jane shyly.

'And why not? But I wonder what happens when you get married—I mean, could you go on being a surgeon and running a house and a husband and children too?'

Jane blushed. 'Well, I don't suppose so.' She added ingenuously: 'I suppose being a surgeon's wife is the next best thing . . .'

'I daresay it is,' agreed Polly kindly, 'and being married to someone who's interested in surgery would make it awfully nice for him to come home to.'

Jane sipped her tea and thought about it. 'I believe you're right. Didn't Diana look lovely?'

Polly nodded. 'And so happy. I like weddings, don't you?'

'Yes, very much. Are you going to get married?'

'Not that I know of,' said Polly lightly.

'Oh, I wondered—that is, I thought perhaps Joseph was yours.'

'No, he's not mine,' said Polly gently. 'We're friends in a casual sort of way and when Professor

Gervis heard that both of us had invitations he suggested that we should come together—we don't know anyone here, you see.'

She watched Jane sigh with relief. 'Joseph wondered if I'd like to see round the hospital one day,' she observed.

'You'll like that, and he could explain everything to you,' Polly put down her cup. 'Here they are now, we'll have to go. Do you live here?'

'In Cheltenham.' Jane looked round vaguely. 'Mother and Father are somewhere here. We're to stay to a family dinner party.'

Most of the guests were leaving now and Polly tapped Joseph's sleeve. 'We have to go, don't we?' she declared. 'My father's coming for me this evening . . .' She gave Joseph's arm a warning nip just in case he said something foolish; he knew as well as she did that she wouldn't be going home, but he was quite capable of voicing surprise.

'Then we mustn't keep you,' said the Professor, so readily that Polly wondered uneasily if they had outstayed their welcome. But he had asked Joseph to go with him to his study. She wished Jane goodbye and walked to the door to pause and bid goodbye to old Mrs Gervis, sitting in a wing chair close by.

'Goodbye, my dear,' said that lady, 'or should it be *au revoir*, I wonder?' She chuckled and Polly smiled politely; she thought it unlikely that they would ever meet again. At the door she paused. Joseph was loitering with Jane, and she couldn't blame him, all the same the Professor would probably want to get away as quickly as possible. She wished him goodbye and thanked him, then turned round to collect Joseph, who took no notice at all, he was too deep in conversation with Jane.

'Young love,' murmured the Professor into her ear. And then, testily: 'Such a silly phrase! Love isn't only for the young; it attacks all ages and at the most awkward times.'

There was nothing Polly could think of in answer to that. She began to walk down the drive to where the Ford stood in shabby isolation, the Professor beside her.

'Don't bother to wait,' she suggested. 'You must want to get back to your guests.'

'You're my guest,' he pointed out.

'You know very well what I mean. Ah, here's Joseph.' She thanked him for a second time and got into the car, then had to wait while Joseph expressed his thanks too. He seemed in no hurry, indeed, he appeared to be waiting for something, and when the Professor made the casual suggestion that instead of driving back to the hospital he should take Polly home, he agreed with alacrity. Polly, listening to them, wanted very much to box their complacent ears. She felt like a parcel to be delivered as conveniently as possible and she said so tartly. They looked at her with indulgence and the Professor explained: 'It's a good idea, isn't it? I shall be travelling back tomorrow evening and will collect you on the way. I'm sure your mother will be delighted to see you and give Joseph some supper.' He clapped Joseph on the shoulder. 'In with you, boy!'

'I have nothing with me,' declared Polly crossly, 'not even a toothbrush.'

'Bound to be a spare one at home,' observed the Professor, and smiled widely at her. 'I'll call for you about seven o'clock—do you suppose your

mother would give me supper, or shall we have
something on the way back?'

'Mother will be delighted,' said Polly, still cross,
resisting the temptation to have dinner with him.
With the entire family round her, it would be
easier. She didn't stop to explain to herself what
would be easier.

The Professor stood back, looking positively
smug, and Joseph shot away towards the village.

'What on earth made him suggest that you should
take me home?' demanded Polly wrathfully.

'No idea. He just said it seemed a good notion
while we were in the study, you know.'

'I might have guessed!'

Joseph gave her a sidelong glance. 'I should
have thought you would have been delighted to go
home.' He sounded aggrieved. 'I'm going out of my
way, but the Professor said . . .'

'Don't tell me, I know what he said.' She saw
Joseph's downcast face and said instantly: 'Oh,
Joseph, how horrid I am—it's good of you to
bring me home and I'm most grateful, perhaps I
can do something in return?'

He seized on that like a dog on a bone. 'Jane
and I,' he began, 'well—we like each. If ever you
get the chance—I mean if you were to see her . . .'

'I'll laud you to the skies and I'll do my best to
have you there if ever we should meet. It's not
likely, but I won't forget. She's sweet, isn't she?
She talked about you, said you were going to take
her round the hospital.'

'Well, I'd have to get Professor Gervis's
permission.'

'That won't be any trouble, he told his Deirdre
that you were going to be a very good surgeon one
day. He sounded proud of you.'

'I say, did he say that?'

At least someone's happy, thought Polly sourly, and was instantly sorry for having such a mean thought.

Everyone was at home when they arrived; Joseph was absorbed into the family with no trouble at all and within an hour of their arrival he was sitting round the table with the rest of them, making inroads into Mrs Talbot's quiche Lorraine and jacket potatoes. Nicely replete with the fruit tart which followed it, he was only too happy to reply to that lady's carefully put questions about Professor Gervis.

'And his fiancée?' prompted Mrs Talbot.

Joseph looked uncomfortable. 'Well, we don't all like the same people, do we?' he wanted to know. 'I mean, she's not quite my cup of tea, but I daresay she's very nice when you get to know her.'

An answer which afforded Mrs Talbot a good deal of satisfaction.

He didn't go until almost ten o'clock, declaring that the evening had been one to remember for a long time. He gave Polly a friendly pat on the shoulder with a careless: 'See you on the ward, Polly,' and added: 'You won't forget, will you?'

'No, Joseph, I won't. And thanks for bringing me back.'

'Well, to be honest, I should never have thought of it, it was Professor Gervis who put the idea into my head.'

Polly spent a good deal of the night wondering why.

She put on an old dress in the morning and went to pick strawberries while Shylock accompanied her in close attendance. 'And you might pop over to Dingle's farm and get some cream, darling,' suggested her mother. 'Do you suppose a bacon and egg pie would do for supper?'

'I don't see why not,' observed Polly. 'If he doesn't like it he can leave it.'

A remark which made her mother pause to look at her. 'You looked very nice yesterday, darling,' she said. 'I suppose you'll have to wear the outfit back this evening.' She added hopefully: 'You might need it.'

'Very unlikely, but I'll have to put it on, I haven't anything else with me.' Polly looked down at the limp cotton dress she was wearing. 'I can't go in this, can I?'

'Certainly not, love. There's only you and me for lunch, shall we have coffee and sandwiches?'

The Professor wasn't mentioned for the rest of the day. After tea Polly changed into the pink skirt and blouse again, did her hair with more care than usual and took pains with her face, so that Cora and Marian professed themselves agreeably surprised.

'I always said you'd look pretty if you took the trouble,' said Cora, and, 'You and your Greek verbs!' observed Marian.

The Professor arrived at exactly seven o'clock and, in some way best known to himself, instantly became one of the family. He was 'Sam' within ten minutes, discussing education with his host, the wedding with his hostess, exchanging badinage with Cora and Marian and listening patiently to Ben's questions about his car. Polly had to admit that towards herself his manner was exactly right; friendly, casual and uninterested.

It was while they were finishing the last of Mrs Talbot's bacon and egg pie that that lady, handing out second helpings, asked in a voice of transparent innocence: 'And you, Sam? When are you getting married?'

Everyone looked at him, except Polly, who looked at her plate.

'I hope very soon, Mrs Talbot. One or two small matters to clear up first, of course, before we can decide on the date.'

'Of course. I hope you'll ask us to the wedding.'

'I can promise you I shall. What a spendid cook you are, Mrs Talbot; it's to be hoped that your daughters follow in your footsteps.'

'Oh, they do, I made sure of that. The way to a man's heart is through his stomach—well, one of the ways!'

They laughed together and presently after coffee he suggested reluctantly that he and Polly should leave.

Sitting beside him was a delight in itself, but finding something to talk about was another matter. Polly tried the weather, the wedding, and the forthcoming publication of Sir Ronald's book, but somehow the conversation petered out each time, and they finished the journey in silence while she tried feverishly to think of some suitable topic about which to talk. It was disconcerting when he said, as they turned into the hospital forecourt:

'Don't try so hard, Polly. We don't need to talk, you know.' He went on easily: 'I'm going to operate on Baby Gibbs tomorrow, would you like to accompany him to theatre? I think you might be interested.'

'I'd like that, but I daresay Sister Bates wouldn't let me.'

He leaned across her and opened the door. 'Well, we'll see, shall we?' He reached behind and got her case. 'Forgive me if I don't get out—I've got a date . . .'

Deirdre, of course. Polly thanked him nicely and got out briskly, her goodnight just as brisk. On the way to her room she wondered why on earth he had gone out of his way to drive her back. Hardly for the pleasure of her company, she decided ruefully. I might just as well have held my tongue for the whole trip, she told herself crossly as she tidied her wedding finery away in the very back of her clothes cupboard.

It was quite late by now, but not too late for her friends to gather round in her room, drinking mugs of tea from the pot they had brewed by the light of a torch because it was well past the time for the home lights to be out. The talk, naturally enough, was of the wedding, especially the women's clothes, and it was an hour later before Polly got herself into bed, too tired by now to think two sensible thoughts together.

And in the morning there was Sister Bates, telling her sharply that she was to take Baby Gibbs to theatre and she was to be sure to get out in time if she felt faint. 'I can't think why Professor Gervis wants you, it's not as though we're short-staffed today.' She shot an inquisitive glance at Polly. 'I suppose he's got his reasons.'

So at half past eight Polly carried Baby Gibbs to the theatre block, in a panic that she would do the wrong thing or make a fool of herself. But she didn't; the anaesthetist was a goodnatured man who showed her what to do and where she should go, and by the time the small creature was carried into the theatre, she had regained her usual good sense.

The operation was a fairly simple one—

Ramstedt's; the anaesthetist had told her something about it before they went into the theatre. Baby Gibbs had a pyloric stenosis and couldn't keep his food down; a small incision would be made into his pyloris and a few hours after the operation he would be feeding again. Minute quantities, of course, but he would be back to normal in a few days.

Polly stood where she had been told to and looked around her. This was where Sam spent so much of his time, and because of that everything was doubly interesting. There seemed to be an inordinate number of people there; several nurses, one of whom she supposed was Theatre Sister, reputedly a dragon of a woman, and a number of figures, gowned and masked as she was, who she took to be students. There was an elderly man standing opposite her too; the theatre technician, the anaesthetist had explained hurriedly. Polly wasn't sure what he did, but she could ask Sister Tutor during lecture.

She felt a tingle of excitement as the Professor came in with his Registrar and Joseph behind him. He wished everyone a good morning, gave her a brief glance, advised Joseph to stand beside him, since he was there to observe, asked Sister politely if she was ready, and picked up his scalpel.

Polly had no idea how she would feel at her first operation. Usually new student nurses didn't go into theatre for quite some time, but any qualms she might have felt were swallowed up in her content at being there, watching Sam. He worked without haste, talking from time to time; explaining what he was doing and why; she marvelled that he was able to do that and operate as well. She wanted to watch every movement he made and strained to hear every word he uttered, but just in time she remembered Sister Bates' urgent instructions; that she was to stay alert for every second so that she could do what anyone there told her to do, at once.

Save for handing a swab or two she had nothing to do. The operation took its normal course. Baby Gibbs, looking incredibly small and white, was put into her arms only moments after the Professor had pulled off his gloves and left the theatre. There was a long list that morning; she had seen it on Sister's desk. She imagined him stretched out comfortably in the surgeons' room relaxing before the next case.

Back in the ward she handed the baby over to Staff Nurse, gave a careful report to Sister, and was told to go for her coffee break, taken up almost entirely but not wholly by excited questions from her friends who hadn't been given the chance of going to theatre yet.

'I wonder why he wanted you there,' someone asked.

'Perhaps he's sweet on you,' said a voice, and everyone laughed. Polly laughed too, wishing with all her heart that it was true.

The Professor came on to the ward later that day, just as she was leaving it to go to lecture with Sister Tutor. She stood aside to allow him to pass and he smiled faintly at her, then turned to speak to Sister Bates; self-assured and elegant, not a hair out of place, exuding a quiet certainty about everything he said and did. It was difficult to remember him sitting at her mother's supper table tucking into bacon and egg pie.

Polly sighed deeply as she made her way through the hospital, already late. Life was getting

difficult and she would have to do something
about it. She had no idea what; she would have to
ponder it well later on; just now she must
concentrate on thinking up a suitable excuse for
her lateness to Sister Tutor.

She was going off duty just after five o'clock,
later than the others because she'd had to go back
to the ward to collect some notes for Sister Tutor,
when she met the Professor. It was an unlikely
place for him to be, in the middle of a rather dark
semi-underground passage between the older part
of the hospital and the new block, and he was
strolling along, with his hands in his pockets,
apparently deep in thought. Polly slowed her steps
when she saw him and for one moment toyed with
the idea of turning tail and going back the way she
had come, but that would have been silly. As they
drew level she gave him a quick look and said,
'Good evening, sir,' in a polite voice, and
quickened her footsteps, only to find that he had
turned round and was walking beside her.

'You're late,' he observed. 'Were you kept in or
something? I promised Grandmother I would take
you back for dinner. She'll be going home in a
couple of days and wants very much to see you
before she does.' He didn't appear to hear Polly's
astonished protest, but glanced at his watch.
'Could you manage half an hour? I'll be at the
entrance.'

She stopped and stared up at him, delight mixed
with annoyance at his high-handed demands. 'I
wasn't going out this evening,' she told him
austerely.

He smiled down at her. 'But now you are. Don't
disappoint an old lady—and if I don't bring you
back with me she'll box my ears!'

Polly laughed. 'Don't be so silly! But I don't quite understand why your grandmother should want to see me again. Is she at your home?'

He nodded. 'Yes, having a rest after all the junketing.' He smiled again, this time with such charm that Polly felt all her good resolutions melting away.

'I was going to bed early,' she began rather feebly.

'You shall sleep in the car,' he promised. They had reached the end of the corridor and there were several people about, going up and down the staircase at its end, looking curiously at them. 'Make it twenty minutes,' he said. 'Please, Polly.'

One of the Office Sisters coming downstairs was looking at them in surprise. Polly said hastily: 'All right, twenty minutes,' and walked away trying to look as though she had merely replied to a polite greeting from one of the consultants; certainly nothing more was expected of her.

She showered and changed with lightning speed, fending off interested enquiries from her friends, telling them with perfect truth that she was going to visit an old lady who particularly wanted to see her that evening. Twenty minutes wasn't long in which to make the most of herself. She put on a plain cotton dress and slung a cardigan around her shoulders, spent a concentrated five minutes on her face and hair and flew back to the front entrance. The Professor was leaning against a radiator, talking to Joseph, and by sheer ill chance, from Polly's point of view, the very same Office Sister crossed the hall as he advanced to meet her. She muttered a good evening to an outraged face and raised eyebrows as she slid past her, and felt a rising indignation at the amusement on the men's faces.

'It's all very well for you to laugh,' she hissed at them. 'I shall be in the Office tomorrow morning, being tried and condemned!'

'What for?' asked the Professor with interest.

'You know quite well—student nurses don't have anything to do with the consultant staff. I must be mad!'

'Don't worry, no one is going to say a word.' He flung an arm round her shoulders and gave them a comforting squeeze. 'I've asked Joseph to bring you to lunch one day next week—Jane will be there . . .'

Polly had given up worrying for the moment. 'Why me? You don't need me there too.'

'Oh, but we do—we can talk to each other and leave the way clear for Joseph to get to know Jane.' He left the radiator and said briskly: 'Well, come along, or there'll be no evening left.' And with a nod to Joseph he whisked her out to the car.

CHAPTER EIGHT

POLLY waited until they were clear of the hospital and weaving through the traffic before she spoke.

'This has to stop, you know,' she said severely, and was thrown off balance by his ready: 'I couldn't agree more. Have you any suggestions?' He slid past a bus and eased the car into the stream of traffic leaving the city. 'You could have refused to come this evening,' his voice was blandly reasonable, 'but then Grandmother would have been disappointed—one shouldn't disappoint the old, don't you agree?'

She sought for an argument and could think of none. 'Yes, well,' she conceded at length, 'but this is the last time,' she said it twice because he didn't answer.

Presently he began to talk about the morning's operation, asking her if she had understood what he had been doing, wanting to know if she had been interested.

'Oh, yes, though there was an awful lot I didn't understand . . .'

'What, for instance?' He encouraged her to question him, and they were still engrossed as he turned the car through the gates of his home, and after that old Mrs Gervis took over, greeting Polly with every sign of pleasure and firing a steady fusillade of questions at her until they went in to dinner.

'Very good of you to come,' she observed in her

resonant voice. 'I daresay you've done a day's work, and to spend your leisure listening to an old lady's ramblings is hardly entertaining.' She shot a look at the Professor at the other end of the table. 'But I daresay that has its compensations.'

They were eating the trifle Jeff had just served them when she said: 'Of course you will visit me, my dear. I live in Cheltenham—perhaps Sam told you? When you can spare the time—? I shall be delighted to see you.'

Polly ate the remains of her trifle and thanked her politely. It seemed unlikely that she would ever see the old lady again, but there was no harm in humouring her. Besides, she liked her, mainly because she was Sam's granny, and anything of his was important to her.

They were sitting in the drawing-room, having their coffee, when Deirdre walked in. The three of them had been talking and laughing and had not heard her car, and they all looked up in surprise as the door was flung open.

'An unexpected pleasure,' said the Professor suavely. 'Do come and join us, Deirdre—I'll get Jeff to bring more coffee. I thought you were dining with the Symes this evening?'

'I left directly after dinner. So this is why you cried off?'

'Yes. I don't often have the pleasure of Grandmother's company and she wanted to meet Polly again before she goes back home.'

Deirdre made a sound which Polly took to be derogatory and sat down. 'Is she spending the night?' she asked spitefully, and nodded towards Polly.

The Professor had resumed his seat and was lying back at his ease, his eyes half hidden under drooping lids. He said very evenly: 'Be careful, Deirdre, Polly is a guest in my house.'

Then she gave a little laugh. 'I wonder what the hospital thinks, although of course I suppose it's usual—affairs between doctors and nurses, it must relieve the boredom.'

He was on his feet. 'I'm not at all sure why you came,' he said silkily, 'but I can see no possible reason for you to stay, Deirdre. I'll see you to your car.'

Something in his face brought her to her feet. 'Don't think I'm going to apologise,' she said to Polly.

'I didn't expect you to,' said Polly in a controlled voice, swamped by Mrs Gervis's decisive tones.

'You need to wash your mouth out with soap and water,' she observed icily. 'If you weren't a guest under Sam's roof I have no doubt he would have bundled you out of the door long since.'

Deirdre stalked to the door, then turned to put a hand on Sam's arm. 'Oh, Sam, I know I've been naughty, but you'll forgive me, won't you? After all, we're to be married soon. You haven't forgotten that?'

She spoke beguilingly and smiled up at him, no trace of bad temper allowed to show.

He moved away so that her hand fell to her side. 'I haven't forgotten, Deirdre.' He opened the door and followed her out into the hall, and presently Polly heard the car start up and be driven away.

'A thoroughly nasty young woman,' said Mrs Gervis sternly. 'Shown in her true colours too.' She smiled at Polly. 'Men,' she declared, 'even the best and cleverest of them, need a helping hand.'

'Here's one that doesn't,' observed the Professor from the door. 'This one is quite capable of managing his own affairs, thank you.'

He crossed the room and sat down again. 'I'm sorry about that, Polly,' and her shocked mind registered the fact that he didn't seem in the least sorry. He went on: 'When are you free next week? Could you spare the time to come to lunch, and if you come with Joseph I'll get Jane up here. I'll run her home in the afternoon and drop you off as we go, if you can manage that?'

So Deirdre and her disgraceful behaviour were to be ignored. She said with her usual calm: 'I've got Thursday and Friday next week . . .'

'Thursday, then. Joseph can drive you here; I'll see he gets his half day. We're operating in the morning—a short list, so he can be away by noon and get here in plenty of time for lunch. I'll go down to Cheltenham and fetch Jane. She's not allowed to drive her own car yet.'

It was on the tip of Polly's tongue to suggest that since it was Joseph who wanted to see Jane again it would be a good idea if he went to Cheltenham to fetch her, but that would mean the Professor having to give her a lift, so she didn't suggest it. She looked up and saw him watching her and coloured faintly, worried that he might have guessed her thoughts. Which, of course, he had.

He drove her back to the hospital an hour later, after a brisk goodbye from his grandmother. 'I shall be seeing you again, my dear,' the old lady said positively. 'It's been a pleasant evening and a very enlightening one'. She offered a soft, elderly cheek. 'You may kiss me.'

Polly sat beside the Professor in the comfort of

the big car. There was a great deal she felt she must say, but how to begin? And he wasn't being helpful, she thought crossly, not saying a word.

'I don't blame Deirdre in the least,' she stated at last, and got stuck. 'What I mean is—she's going to marry you . . . And I meant what I said; this has got to stop . . .'

He eased the Bentley to a gentler pace. 'There are some things on this earth which cannot be stopped, Polly. The tides of the sea, the winds, the changing of the seasons—and falling in love. We are powerless against all these!'

'You're in love with Deirdre,' Polly spoke stubbornly, 'and she's in love with you; you're going to get married.'

'So you keep telling me, dear girl. Have you ever been in love, Polly?'

It was easy to talk to him in the summer dusk, their faces in the dim car. 'Once,' she told him soberly, and didn't add for all time, for she knew that was true, she would never love anyone quite as she loved him; once he was married she would make herself get over it; it had been done before by other women, so she would do it too. He was perhaps a little interested—if not in love—with her, and that was why he and Deirdre were at odds. Before she had met him that day on the way home, his future must have looked settled and happy, and somehow, without wishing to, she had unsettled him. She said out loud without meaning to: 'Oh, you must get married soon, Sam.'

He laughed softly. 'Oh, I intend to.' He pulled into the side of the road and stopped. 'You called me Sam,' he observed mildly and leaned over to kiss her, not mildly at all. He drove on again at once, saying nothing, whistling under his breath, while Polly, wordless, sat beside him.

At the hospital he said: 'I'll be away for a few days, but I'll fix things with Joseph for next Thursday.' He got out and opened her door and went with her into the entrance hall, where he wished her goodnight in the friendliest casual way, then went to speak to the night porter about something or other.

Polly mumbled thanks and a goodnight and hurried over to the Home, hoping her friends would be in their beds so that she could get into her own bed quickly and think things out. But they were still milling around, making a last mug of tea, grumbling about aching feet and hardhearted Ward Sisters and staff nurses. They pounced on Polly, offered tea and settled down to question her about her evening.

'Was she tiresome, this old lady?' one of her friends asked. 'You look all in, Polly.'

'Actually, she's rather an old dear, but I suppose I was tired to start with and she asked a great many questions. But I do like her.'

They all went to their beds presently and Polly had a long very hot bath which didn't clear her head at all, only made her sleepy. She got into bed presently and fell asleep, her thoughts in such a tangle she had no idea how to start unravelling them.

Nothing went right the next day. Staff, who had taken a dislike to her anyway, kept pouncing on her, finding fault with the smallest thing, and to make matters worse she tripped up with a bowl of water in the middle of the ward and sent the contents in all directions, just at the very moment that the Professor came in. It was a splendid opportunity for Staff to bawl her out in her ladylike tones, highlighting the unfortunate episode for everyone excepting Polly's benefit, but the Professor didn't appear to notice or hear anything amiss. He turned his back and walked to the other end of the ward, deep in consultation with his Registrar and Joseph, and stayed engrossed in his small patients until Polly had taken herself and her mop out of the ward.

And Sister Tutor, usually a long-suffering though stern woman, grumbled at her; her notes had been badly written, and by now she should know the bones of the body—and she a Latin scholar, and her case history of a child with whooping cough was far too scrimpy. Polly ended her day convinced that she was never going to be good at anything; she'd end up as a mother's help or a companion to some old woman. She wasn't sure if there were still companions about, one never heard of them these days, but they just happened to suit her remarkably depressed spirits. Tomorrow, she decided, getting ready for bed, no longer bolstered up by her friends and mugs of tea, she would go to the office and ask to leave.

Nine o'clock was the time appointed for nurses to go to the Office, either to make requests for themselves or to be lectured for a crime so heinous that Ward Sister was incapable of dealing with it. She would have to get permission from Sister Bates, of course, and Polly kept an eye on the clock while she cleaned up the toddlers after their breakfast, only to be stymied at the last minute by the abrupt departure of Sister from the ward. Staff was in X-Ray, getting some necessary films, and Nurse Honeybun was bathing babies. Of the other two nurses, one had gone to change her apron after a disastrous episode with a bowl of porridge and the other one had days off. Polly, having screwed up her courage, felt let down. She tied a clean bib round the last toddler and started to walk towards Sister's Office on the landing, glancing with pardonable pride at the row of clean little faces in their cots. Only in the last cot of all, the small face wasn't only clean, it was a nasty blue colour as well.

Polly gave a small yelp of alarm; she'd been told about asphyxia, but she hadn't seen it before. It would be of no use calling for Nurse Honeybun, busy with a baby in its bath; she would have to do something. Polly plucked the child from its cot and held it up by the heels, then slapped it gently between its tiny shoulder blades, nothing happened, indeed the blue deepened and its breaths were alarmingly infrequent. Over the first shock, Polly remembered what else she had been told to do. She righted the toddler and poked a careful finger down its throat. There was nothing there, not to be reached anyway. With calm desperation she ran through the ward with the child in her arms, out of the swing doors across the landing and into the forbidden domain of theatre.

There were several people in the vestibule leading to the anaesthetic room. She thrust the child at the one nearest—the Professor.

'Sam,' she cried, 'for heaven's sake—he's not breathing! I've held him upside down and put a finger down his throat—do something!'

There was a profound silence for a couple of seconds—on account of the child, but also because no one there had ever dared to call Professor Gervis Sam to his face. He didn't say a word, merely put the child on the examination table and bent over it. Polly waited long enough to hear him say: 'A scalpel and a trachiostomy tube, if you please,' before she raced back to the ward to encounter Staff's outraged face.

'How dare you leave the ward, Nurse Talbot—it's absolutely forbidden, and you know it! Nurse Honeybun can't be here there and in the baby's room—you're quite irresponsible!'

'Benny Miles,' said Polly. 'He was choking—there wasn't anyone here, I didn't know what to do. I ran to theatre with him . . .'

Staff swelled up like a turkeycock. 'You what?' she demanded. 'You know you may never go there unless you have permission, and there's a list this morning. I shall report you to Sister. Where is Benny?'

'In theatre. Professor Gervis was looking after him.'

'Stay in the ward and don't dare leave it. I'm going to theatre. You're quite untrustworthy, Nurse Talbot.'

It had only needed something like that to happen, thought Polly. She hadn't the least idea what else she should have done, but quite obviously she had done the wrong thing. If she hadn't already made up her mind to go to the office this had clinched the matter for her. The moment Sister Bates came through the door she asked to go and speak to the Principal Nursing Officer, remembering to add: 'Staff's in Theatre with Benny Miles—he's asphyxiated, Sister.' Then she scuttled away before Sister could start her questions. There was exactly five minutes left of the time allowed for nurses to go to the Office each morning, and although her hair was untidy and her apron was rumpled, she really didn't care. Indignation and fright had superimposed themselves on any other feelings. Only at the back of her mind she felt relief that it had been Sam there; he'd know what to do and Benny would be all right again.

She was the last there and the Office Sister frowned at her. 'Nurse, you're very untidy, I suggest you come tomorrow morning at nine o'clock,' her stern eye pinpointed the clock on the wall, showing barely two minutes to go, 'and come tidily dressed, please.'

'I got held up,' said Polly earnestly, 'and I really must see Miss Brice, it's very urgent.'

The Office Sister sniffed. 'Very well, you may go in, Nurse—what's your name?'

'Talbot, Sister.' Polly opened the door and crossed the Office to stand before the desk. The last time she had done that she reflected, was at her interview, such a short time ago.

'Nurse Talbot?' The Principal Nursing Officer looked at her, smiling a little. She knew all about Polly and Professor Gervis, seen talking by an outraged Office Sister; she knew about a good deal more than that too, but she liked the Professor, they were friends of long standing, and she had nothing against the rather plain and at the moment tense girl in front of her.

Polly drew a breath. 'Miss Brice, I should like to leave. I—I'm not good enough to be a nurse—I'm irresponsible and I break rules and I drop things.' She thought for a moment. 'Oh, and I'm untrustworthy.'

Miss Brice settled back in her chair. 'And who says these things, Nurse?'

'Oh, well, I couldn't tell you that, Miss Brice, but it's quite true.' She added in a calm little voice: 'I've made up my mind. I'm sorry because I thought . . . I've been told by someone who is an authority on—on nursing that I would never be a nurse.'

'Have you really thought about this, Nurse? It's not just a sudden flash in the pan because something's gone wrong on the ward? You're with Sister Bates, aren't you?'

'Yes, Miss Brice, and Sister's been very kind.'

'And you still want to leave?'

'Yes, I do. Do I have to wait a whole month?'

Miss Brice studied Polly's pale face. 'No,' she said gently, 'that won't be necessary, but you do understand that I must have a report from your Ward Sister first, don't you? I think the best thing is for you to take your days off as from now—I'll see Sister Bates, you have no need to go back to the ward—go home and talk it over with your parents and make a final decision. Let's see, it's Tuesday—report here on Thursday after lunch, Nurse, and if you still wish to go we can arrange matters then.'

'Yes, Miss Brice. I can go home now?'

'Just as soon as you've changed. I'll see you on Thursday, then.'

Polly left by a side entrance and caught a bus to the station. There were trains enough to Cheltenham, she took the next one and then caught a bus to Pulchester and then another local one to her home. Her mother was the only one there. She took a quick look at Polly's face and said cheerfully: 'Darling, what a lovely surprise! Come into the kitchen and I'll make another pot of coffee.'

Polly's frozen face crumpled. 'Oh, Mother!' she mumbled, and burst into tears.

The Professor straightened his long back and

threw a small brass bell—the kind worn by teddy bears—into the kidney dish a nurse was holding out. 'Touch and go,' he commented. 'Leave the tube in for twenty-four hours and then I'll have him back and close the wound. Where's Nurse Talbot?'

'Gone back to the ward,' said a voice, and he nodded.

'Keep him here in the Recovery Room until he's O.K.' He glanced round him. 'Ah, there's Staff Nurse from the ward. Joseph, give her the details. I'm going to scrub. And tell her to see there aren't any more bells lying round for the children to swallow.'

He had a heavy list, it was almost one o'clock when he left the theatre, and went into the ward to look at his small patients. The ward was busy now and noisy as his four morning cases came round from their anaesthetics. He spent some time with them and then strolled round the cots and little beds until he reached Benny, back in his own cot again, sleeping peacefully.

The Professor glanced around him. 'Where's Nurse Talbot? She deserves some thanks for acting so promptly this morning.'

Sister Bates hesitated. 'If you'd come into my office for a moment, Professor . . .'

He didn't ask any questions, only waited while she sat down at her desk.

'Miss Brice telephoned. Nurse Talbot went to see her this morning—directly after she left the theatre—and she asked to leave. She's gone home for two days to think it over and will report back on Thursday afternoon.'

'Why?'

'She told Miss Brice that she had been told that

she would never be a nurse, that she dropped things, that she was untrustworthy, irresponsible and broke the rules. She has quite made up her mind. I was asked to give a report and I've said she has the makings of a good nurse. She's a natural with children, she's honest and punctual and tries really hard.'

'Who told her she was untrustworthy? Who was in the ward when she came back from theatre?'

Sister Bates looked awkward. 'Staff Nurse. When I got back she'd gone to theatre, of course, and Nurse Talbot was here alone.'

The Professor sat down on the edge of the desk. 'Would you get Staff Nurse Stockley, please. I'll speak to her here.'

Sister Bates lifted the phone. 'She'll be in the dining room. She's a bit hard on the young ones, but she doesn't mean to be unkind.'

She would have said more than that, but her companion's mouth was set so grimly that she remained silent until Staff Nurse tapped on the door and came in. It surprised her when Sister Bates went out after the brief observation that Professor Gervis wanted a word with her, but she turned a smile on him; he might be an engaged man, but there was never any harm in turning on the charm.

'What exactly did you say to Nurse Talbot?' he asked with silky politeness. 'And I would like the exact words. You accused her of leaving the ward, perhaps?'

She bridled. 'Indeed I did, sir. She had no right to leave the children alone, and I told her so.'

'Yes? And what else did you say to her?' His voice was so mild that she went on readily:

'I pointed out that she was untrustworthy and

irresponsible and forever breaking rules—she's quite unsuitable as a nurse, you know.'

'Suppose you leave that for others to judge, Staff Nurse? And if ever I hear of you speaking in that way to any other student nurse, there will be trouble.' He got off the desk and towered over her. 'I'm very angry. You'd better go now.'

She went, and he stayed where he was after she had gone, staring out of the window at the rooftops around him. Presently he walked unhurriedly down the ward, bade Sister Bates a civil goodbye and went downstairs to Miss Brice's office.

Mrs Talbot didn't try to stop Polly crying. She made the coffee, sat down at the table beside her daughter, offered a hanky and waited. Presently Polly sniffed, blew her nose and took a gulp of coffee. 'I'm going to leave, Mother. I'm no good as a nurse, really I'm not. I've loved it, but Sam said I'd never be a nurse, and he's right—I should have stuck to Greek and Latin!'

Mrs Talbot with unerring maternal instinct, hit the right nail on the head. 'Sam—Sam said that?' She stared at the wall and began to smile.

Polly didn't see the smile. 'I tripped up and spilt a bowl of water just as he came to do a round—there's a simply beastly staff nurse, and then Benny choked . . .'

'Have some more coffee,' invited her mother, 'and start at the beginning, darling.'

Polly sucked in her lower lip like a child and began. When she had finished her mother said comfortably: 'Well, you have two days to think about it, love, but take my advice and don't dwell on it too much, just potter about and take Shylock for his walk and do a bit of gardening; sometimes things look different when you've put time and distance between you.'

She got up and took the coffee cups to the sink. 'You pop upstairs and do your face and I'll make some sandwiches, we'll have them in the garden and perhaps you'd pop down to the village presently and get a few things from Mrs Greggs.'

When Polly had gone upstairs, her mother sat down again at the table. 'I'd better be prepared,' she murmured thoughtfully. 'If I make a really big steak and kidney pie—there are peas enough in the garden, and courgettes, and strawberries and cream for afters.' She nodded her head. 'Polly can bring back some more cheese, and I'll make a cake and some cheese straws . . .'

She started cutting bread, looking pleased with herself.

Polly came down presently, nose and eyes still a little red, but with her face done and her hair a smooth curtain once more. She had changed into one of her cotton dresses, well washed and a little faded, and put sandals on to bare feet. She looked like a little girl, only her eyes looked huge and sad in her still pale face.

By teatime, though, she looked better, for there was colour in her cheeks from the long walk she had taken Shylock and her nose was no longer even faintly pink. She even ate quite a good tea before going into the garden to pick the strawberries with Ben, and then, at her mother's request, getting on her bike to fetch the cream.

They had all been dears, she mused, pedalling along briskly through the lanes. If they had been surprised they hadn't shown it, nor had they asked a lot of stupid questions. Of course, she would

have to explain to her father later; he'd asked her
to check some Latin papers with him and that
would be as good a time as any.

She collected the cream, passed the time of day
with Mrs Coffin, and pedalled briskly back home.
It was a glorious evening, very quiet save for the
country sounds around her. Perhaps Sam had been
right after all; she wasn't a town girl, she would do
better to stay at home. She turned in at the open
gate. The Bentley was crouching majestically
before the door.

Polly, braking so hard that she almost fell off,
drew a loud, indignant breath, sprinted to the back
door, propped the bike against the wall and went
in. There was the tail end of her mother's skirt
whisking through the kitchen door into the hall
and she was alone with the Professor, sitting very
much at his ease on the edge of the kitchen table.

Neither mincing her words nor stopping to
think, Polly began: 'If you've come to tell me I'm
not to leave, you're wasting your time.'

His dark eyes studied her flushed face. 'Oh,
dear, oh dear, you are cross,' he observed mildly,
'and all for nothing. You have my full support if
you want to go—it's the most sensible thing
you've decided upon in weeks.'

The ground cut from under her feet, she stood
goggling at him. 'You really meant it—that I
would never be a nurse?' She lifted her chin
defiantly. 'Then why are you here, Professor?'

'Sam,' he said, still mild. 'We shall have to have
that little talk, Polly, but you ran away.'

Her voice rose despite her efforts to present an
untroubled front. 'I did not—I most certainly did
not!' There seemed to be no point in going on.

He got off the table and came and stood in front

of her. 'Benny's better,' he said. 'He owes his life to you. Never mind the rubbish Staff Nurse Stockley told you. You did exactly what any sensible girl would have done.'

Polly's eyes filled with tears; she was unhappy and uncertain and no longer thinking straight. 'Oh, I am glad he's all right!'

'Does that make you change your mind?'

She wiped away the tears with a furious hand. 'No, it doesn't. Oh, go home to your Deirdre, do!'

He smiled a little at that and took her hands in his. 'Yes, I must do that presently, but first there is something that I must say to you.'

His hands felt very comforting, but she tried not to think of them. 'About Deirdre?'

'Yes.' He let go of one of her hands and ran a gentle finger down her cheek. 'I'm not usually at a loss for words, but I think I'm going to find this . . .'

He was interrupted by Mrs Talbot's voice from the door. 'So sorry, but Sam, you're wanted urgently—it's the hospital. The telephone's in the hall.'

He went without a word, and Polly, standing in the kitchen with her mother, could hear his voice, curt and brisk. A minute later he came back into the kitchen. 'I must go at once. I'm sorry, Mrs Talbot.' He looked at Polly, standing exactly as he had left her. 'I'll come back as soon as I can.' He had gone before she could get her mouth open; she heard the Bentley go down the drive and up the hill, on its urgent way to Birmingham.

'Ah, well,' said Mrs Talbot regretfully, 'we'll have a nice quiet evening.' And Polly, never more mistaken in her life, agreed.

They were still in the kitchen dishing up the supper when she heard a car turn in at the gate. She stopped mashing the potatoes, her pale face suddenly pink and happy. It took only seconds to realise that it couldn't possibly be Sam; someone for Cora or Marian, she supposed, and went back to her mashing.

Cora put her head round the kitchen door, her face surprised and a little worried, and she paused again. 'It's Sam's . . . she says she's Deirdre and wants to see you, Polly.'

Polly put the saucepan back on the stove, wiped her hands and said: 'Don't wait for me, Mother, everything will spoil and I shan't be more than a minute or two.' Then she crossed the hall to the sitting room. Deirdre was alone; everyone else was in the garden and she was standing at the window watching them. She turned round as Polly went in and took a few steps towards her. Her glance invited Polly to compare the two of them—she in an elegant silky outfit which must have cost the earth, not a hair out of place, Polly in her cotton dress and sandals, and her hair not all that tidy. The glance had been calculated to put Polly at a disadvantage, but it left her unworried but puzzled. She said: 'Hullo?' on a questioning note, and Deirdre said quickly:

'Sam said you'd be here—he's been, hasn't he? He told me he was coming.' She paused and smiled with gentle malice. 'Actually we arranged to meet here.'

Polly didn't ask why. 'He was called away unexpectedly, to the hospital, I think, but he didn't say . . .'

The other girl fiddled with a bracelet and Polly wondered why she was nervous.

'He didn't talk to you, then.'

'No.' For the life of her, Polly couldn't have said any more. There was a lump of ice inside her, getting bigger and bigger every moment. She wasn't sure why, only that she was suddenly full of dire forebodings.

Deirdre gave a tinkling laugh. 'Oh, well, I suppose I'll have to tell you—Sam wanted to keep it a secret from everyone, but I insisted that we must tell you. You've been seeing quite a lot of him, haven't you, and we began to think . . .' She paused and laughed again. 'Well, you know how it sometimes is—you may have mistaken his interest in you.'

She watched Polly's pale face flush, well pleased. 'Sam is so interested in people—he wanted to see how you would make out as a nurse. He was so certain you wouldn't finish your training—not the type, too . . .' she paused again: 'countryfied explains it, I suppose, and too wrapped up in Greek and Latin.'

She waited for Polly to speak and when she didn't: 'You've no idea what Sam was going to say to you?' she asked sharply.

'No,' said Polly quietly, and thought that wasn't quite true. She had hoped—well, when he'd been talking to her a tiny flame had begun to flicker, too small for her to feel more than a vague excitement at what he was going to say. The flame flickered now and died. She had her face nicely under control when Deirdre went on: 'We're getting married in two days' time, very quietly. I wanted a big wedding, but Sam says he won't wait any longer. Of course, Mother and Father are furious—I'm the only one, you know, and they wanted a big affair.' She stared at Polly. 'Did Sam say he was coming back?'

'Yes.'

'Oh, well, I'll tell him he needn't bother now—you don't need to see him again, do you? I'll tell him all the usual things, shall I? Congratulations and so on. I must be going—we're dining out.' She sniffed delicately. 'There's a frightful smell of cooking—I suppose it's your supper. You must have found living in Sam's house very different from this.' Her eyes took her in and the comfortable shabbiness of the pleasant room.

Polly didn't answer that. She went to the door and opened it, then led the way across the hall and pushed the half open front door wide. And when Deirdre was outside she shut it again; she heard Deirdre's indignant snort at such cavalier treatment.

She leaned against the door, listening to the car being driven away, then walked slowly into the dining room. They all looked at her pinched pale face and her mother said: 'Come and sit down, love,' and started to put food on to a plate.

Polly sat obediently, accepted the plate and pushed its contents round without eating anything. Presently she said in an expressionless voice: 'Sam's getting married in two days' time. Deirdre came to tell me. That's why he came to see me, he said he had something to tell me . . .'

Her father spoke. 'I imagine Sam will return. If he wanted to tell you this himself—he's that kind of man.'

Mrs Talbot started to collect up the plates and Cora took them out to the kitchen and everyone made small talk while they ate the strawberries and cream, and when they'd finished Cora and Marian offered to wash up and Ben went away to do his homework.

'You'll want to talk to your mother,' said Mr Talbot, and left them there still sitting at the table.

'You don't have to talk about it, love,' said Mrs Talbot, 'but is there anything we can do to help—do you want to do anything?'

'I don't want to see Sam again,' said Polly slowly. 'You see, I love him very much and I couldn't bear it if he found out. Deirdre said he wouldn't come back—there was no need, but I'm not sure about that. Mother, could I go to Aunt Maggie's? Just for a week or two. I've got enough money for the fare.'

'I don't see why not, darling. Shall you write to her?'

'I'll ring her up—now. I can catch the early morning bus to Birmingham from the village and catch the ten-thirty from there—the one you and Father caught last year.'

'You'll have to change at Crewe,' said her mother faintly. 'Must you go so quickly, Polly?'

'Yes, Mother—please. You see, when I come back Sam will be married and it'll be over and done with.' She sighed. 'It was silly of me, wasn't it, to fall in love with someone who's never given me so much as a second glance.' She got up and set her chair neatly in its place. 'I'll ring Aunt Maggie now and pack a bag.'

CHAPTER NINE

It was half past six and full daylight by the time Sam stretched his back, stood while the nurse untied his gown, stripped off mask and gloves and left the theatre. He had operated throughout the night on the small battered bodies which had been brought out of the ruins of a tenement block, and now he gave careful instructions to his Registrar, bade everyone a pleasant good morning and went to the consultants' room. Presently he would shower and shave, but now he needed to sleep for an hour.

By eight o'clock he was his usual elegant self, eating breakfast with Joseph and the Registrar, and half an hour later he was back on the ward, checking his patients of the night and doing a round, unworried by the chaos of breakfasts, baths and treatments.

'I shall be away for the rest of the day,' he told his Registrar. 'Get Mr Toms if you're worried but you can reach me after six o'clock at my home—if I'm not there Jeff will know where I am.' He checked on his way out of the ward. 'Joseph, I'd almost forgotten—Jane is coming to lunch tomorrow, isn't she? Well, that's still on, though I think we'll have to rearrange things. I'll give you a ring this evening. It's a short list in the morning, there should be enough time.'

Joseph grinned. 'Yes, sir. But what about Polly—someone said she'd left.'

'She'll be there, Joseph,' said the Professor imperturbably.

He left the hospital and got into the Bentley, and half an hour later he was at the Talbots' house.

Mrs Talbot met him at the open front door. 'Sam! Deirdre said you weren't coming back.' Her eyes searched his impassive face. 'You're tired—you've been up all night, of course—that block of flats with all those children sleeping.'

He smiled faintly. 'Where's Polly, Mrs Talbot?'

She said in a whisper: 'Gone to Scotland. Oh, Sam, Deirdre said . . .'

He took her gently by the arm. 'Deirdre seems to have said a good deal. Perhaps you would tell me about it.'

'Yes—oh yes, of course, Sam. Come into the kitchen and we'll have coffee.'

As she filled the mugs he asked: 'Why Scotland?'

'It was as far away as she could go . . .'

He laughed then, a bitter laugh, so that Mrs Talbot's tongue was betrayed into exclaiming: 'She loves you, Sam, that's why she had to go away. She couldn't bear to be here, knowing that you and Deirdre are going to marry.'

He put down his mug. 'I think perhaps you might tell me exactly what happened, Mrs Talbot.'

It took quite a time, for Mrs Talbot was worried and upset and kept adding bits she had forgotten, but finally Sam spoke. 'I'll find her at Crewe.' He glanced at his watch. 'There's half an hour to wait there, you say? I should make it easily. But first let me set your mind at rest, Mrs Talbot. Deirdre and I broke off our engagement before Diana's wedding, although we said nothing as I didn't want

Diana's day to be spoilt.' He got to his feet, looking down at her. 'I'm going to marry Polly, if she'll have me.' He bent and kissed Mrs Talbot's cheek. 'You'll make a delightful mother-in-law.'

At the door he turned to smile at her. 'We'll ring you later.'

Mrs Talbot found her voice. 'Sam, you're tired to death, you can't drive all that way—it's too far!'

'Never too far to be with my Polly,' he told her.

Polly sat wedged between an old man with a bad cough and a fat lady who wanted to talk. The bus to Birmingham had been late getting in and she had had to hurry to catch the train to Crewe, so unexpectedly full that she had given up looking for a window seat and at the last minute insinuated her small person between her neighbours. It was already quite warm and the boy opposite her was smoking endlessly, so it was a relief when she recognised the outskirts of Crewe.

The station was crowded with people milling around the platforms, so it took a few minutes to get herself and her case from the train and over the bridge to the right platform. The train was running a little late, a muffled voice over the Tannoy told her, so she took herself off to the buffet. A cup of coffee would pass the time, and something to eat. She had had almost no breakfast, despite her mother's gentle nagging, and now she felt famished. The journey ahead would be lengthy and she supposed that somewhere on the way she would have to eat; it would be late by the time she reached Aunt Maggie's and she couldn't expect that lady, however goodnatured, to cook a hot meal for her.

Just for a moment she wished most desperately to be home again—indeed, the feeling was so

strong that she might have picked up her case
and gone back over the bridge and caught the
next train back to Birmingham, only by now
there was a solid queue behind her, and those in
front were already at the buffet counter. She got
her coffee and what looked like a plastic
sandwich wrapped in more plastic and went to
sit at one of the crowded tables. There were five
other people there; a youngish woman with two
toddlers, an elderly lady in a disastrous hat and
three important-looking men with briefcases.
They were talking together in low voices and
scarcely looked at her, the toddlers were crying
while their mother drank her coffee, taking no
notice of them at all, only the elderly lady
looked her over slowly and then went on
drinking. Polly, sipping her own tasteless drink,
began, quite against her intention, thinking
about Sam. Tomorrow would be his wedding
day—and that reminded her suddenly that that
was to have been the day when Joseph and Jane
were to have had lunch with him. She supposed
they would go to the wedding instead; after all,
Deirdre would have to have a few guests,
however quiet the occasion was to be.

Polly, in her mind's eye, saw the girl, draped in
the very latest fashion, standing beside Sam in the
village church. The picture was so vivid that she
felt the tears prick her eyelids. What a fool she had
been—she should have stuck to her Latin and
Greek. She blew her nose vigorously and gave the
elderly lady a defiant look.

The three business men were getting ready to go,
but she didn't look up at the small commotion
they made. Sam's voice, very gentle in her ear,
turned her giddy for the moment.

'What,' he asked, 'is that revolting thing on the table?'

'A s-sandwich.'

Sam picked it up and looked at it closely. 'Someone should write to *The Times* about it,' he observed, and smiled at the elderly lady who, taken aback, smiled in return. The toddlers were still crying, but he ignored them. 'The car's outside,' he said to Polly, and took her shaking hand in his. And then: 'I said I'd come back, my darling.'

Polly sought for words and because she couldn't find any to fit the occasion, looked at him. He was smiling a little, watching her intently, but tired lines were etched in his face still.

'Sam,' she said uncertainly, 'I don't believe you've had any sleep—you look all in. And why are you here? Tomorrow's your wedding day.'

It hurt to say that, but she felt better when she had.

'No, it's not. Tomorrow we're entertaining Joseph and Jane to lunch, or had you forgotten?'

'But Deirdre said . . .' And then: 'How did you know where I was?'

He ignored the elderly lady, who had bent forward a little so that she could hear what they were saying.

'Your mother told me. Polly, darling Polly, Deirdre and I broke off our engagement before Diana got married, but I insisted that we kept quiet about it so that it wouldn't spoil her day.' He took her other hand in his and smiled at her so tenderly that she felt weak inside. 'I knew I could never marry her. One look at you, earnestly telling me to have a cup of coffee, and I was lost.'

'But I'm going to Scotland . . .'

'Another time, dearest girl. We'll go together—a splendid place for a honeymoon.' He glanced across at the elderly lady, taking in every word. 'Don't you agree, madam?' he asked her.

The elderly lady looked surprised. 'Me? You're asking me?' she wanted to know. 'Bless you both, I couldn't think of a better place to go.'

She got up reluctantly and walked away, pausing to look back before she disappeared into the crowd. Polly chuckled. 'Sam, how could you? I mean, we've never seen her before.' She remembered something. 'You said I'd never make a nurse, and I dropped that bowl . . .'

'Of course you'll never be a nurse. You'll have more than enough on your hands with me to look after and the children to bring up.'

'But you didn't like me—you said . . .'

He bent and kissed her very gently, which made the young woman stare. 'Oh, but I did—I loved you to distraction, and it's getting worse every minute. But at first I didn't quite believe it, so I made a kind of smoke-screen of ill humour and of coldness.' He said quietly: 'I've been so very afraid of losing you, my pretty.'

Polly gave a little choking laugh. 'Dear Sam—I didn't like you at first, you know, and then I discovered that I loved you.'

'So you decided to be a nurse and forget me?'

The young woman stubbed a half-smoked cigarette in her saucer and went away, dragging the still howling children with her.

Polly looked down at the large, firm hand holding hers so gently. 'I could never forget you,' she said very softly.

The hand tightened and she felt a pleasant tingle of excitement.

'I shall take care you don't,' said the Professor firmly. 'And here's something to think about until we can go somewhere quiet.'

He put an arm round her and held her close and kissed her thoroughly.

'Sam,' said Polly weakly, 'we're in the middle of Crewe Station.'

He looked around him. 'So we are. I thought it was paradise.' Such a satisfactory answer that she kissed him back.

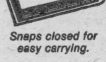